To my neighbor
Julie:
Hope you enjoy this
bit of romance, suspense,
and action.

Evie Lehrer

Phone Tag

A Novel

Evie Lehrer

iUniverse, Inc.
New York Bloomington

Phone Tag
A Novel

iUniverse books may be ordered through booksellers or by contacting:

iUniverse
1663 Liberty Drive
Bloomington, IN 47403
www.iuniverse.com
1-800-Authors (1-800-288-4677)

Because of the dynamic nature of the Internet, any Web addresses or links contained in this book may have changed since publication and may no longer be valid. The views expressed in this work are solely those of the author and do not necessarily reflect the views of the publisher, and the publisher hereby disclaims any responsibility for them.

ISBN: 978-1-4401-2227-9 (pbk)
ISBN: 978-1-4401-2229-3 (cloth)
ISBN: 978-1-4401-2228-6 (ebk)

Printed in the United States of America

iUniverse rev. date: 4/13/2009

Prologue

It was a light day at the hospital. Melanie gave her patient an injection and plumped her pillow. She made an entry on the chart, adjusted her I.V., then returned to the desk. The nurses were chattering about the new intern's long hair. "I wonder what will happen when the administrator sees him. I'll bet he'll make him get a haircut. What do you think Mel?"

"What do I think about what?" Melanie asked absent mindedly as she added some items to the to-do list she was making.

Celia, one of the nurses, realized Melanie was distracted. "What's going on Mel? Are you cooking up something special for the weekend?"

Melanie laughed. "That's exactly what I'm doing. I'm putting together an anniversary dinner for Matt tonight. It's also a celebration of his sobriety, and I want to make it really special."

Celia nodded. "I understand kiddo. Hey, there's not much going on today. I don't mind covering the end of your shift so you can get out of here early." Melanie gratefully accepted Celia's offer. She stopped at the grocery store and picked up a loaf of sour-dough French bread, than went over to the greeting card counter. Most of the anniversary cards were for married couples, but she finally found one for Matt with just the right sentiment, than headed home.

Melanie unlocked her apartment and put her package and briefcase on the kitchen table. Hero, her furry Calico cat, was curled up in a ball on the sofa with one paw resting on his nose. The cat yawned and uncurled, than stood up and arched his back. He reached one white paw out in a feline stretch, than went over to greet Melanie with a "meow-meow." Melanie laughed at his double greeting. She'd never heard Hero meow just once. She picked him up and petted his soft head, and he purred loudly in response. Hero was a rare male Calico. Most Calico cats are female. Their coat color is a sex-linked trait, but Hero was born with one Y and two X chromosomes which produced the beautiful orange and black splotches on his white fur.

Melanie put the cat down and opened a can of tuna. Hero heard the can opener and brushed back and forth against Melanie's leg. She poured the juice and a few pieces of tuna into a bowl. "Look Hero, your favorite treat. I'll eat the rest for lunch tomorrow." Hero lapped at the tuna, a welcome change from the kibble that was his usual diet. Melanie seasoned the rib roast, put it in the oven, and set two russet potatoes on the lower rack to pre-bake. Grabbing her keys, she went into the hall and got her mail. It was all bills and ads. She tossed them on her desk and turned on her computer. Her monthly report needed several entries, but she found it hard to concentrate. She finally gave up and closed the file.

"I want tonight to be perfect," Melanie daydreamed as she showered. "After dinner, we'll put on the old Nat King Cole record and dance. The dishes can wait until morning." She towel-dried her hair, arranging the tawny curls around her face with her fingers. Looking through her closet, she chose the navy blue jumpsuit Matt had given her for her birthday. The hood, with its dark green lining, draped gracefully around her shoulders, bringing out the green in her eyes. She loved the suit, and would have chosen it herself had she seen it in the store. Matt always seemed to know just what she liked, and she cherished the gifts he'd bought for her.

It was 5:30, just enough time to prepare the rest of the dinner and set the table. Melanie sang, "When I fall in love, it will be forever, or I'll never fall in love," as she scooped the potatoes into a bowl, and mashed and seasoned them. She refilled the shells with the mixture, than turned to Hero, "These just need to brown a few minutes. They'll be delicious with a dab of sour cream and chives." She often talked to the cat when Matt wasn't home. Hero was a good listener, and his expressive ears and waving tail told Melanie on no uncertain terms if he didn't agree with what she'd said.

The thermometer in the rib roast registered rare. "Good, it'll be done just the way Matt likes it when he gets home." She threw a cream-colored tablecloth on the table, setting it with her good silverware and china. The two crystal cat holders on the table cradled vanilla-scented candles, also a gift from Matt.

At six, Melanie took everything out of the oven. She cut off a small slice of roast. It was perfectly done, and she popped it into her mouth. "Yum, that's delicious—juicy and tender." Melanie brought the anniversary card to the table and wrote an affectionate message, signed "Love, Melanie," and put it at Matt's place. She lit the candles, dimmed the light in the dining room, and put on some romantic piano music.

The grandfather clock said 6:30. Melanie's stomach tightened. Matt had promised to be home on time. He knew how important this dinner was to them. Struggling to keep a positive attitude, she tore off a piece of foil to cover the roast. She put it, and the potatoes back into the still-warm oven. She added some anchovies to the Ceasar dressing, and sprinkled some parmesan cheese and croutons on the romaine lettuce, waiting to toss it until the last minute. She put the asparagus in the steamer, and draped a napkin in a basket to hold the bread.

"Well, Hero, everything's ready. Now where do you suppose Matt is?" Hero picked up the aggravation in Melanie's voice. His ears flattened and his tail batted back and forth. The phone rang and Melanie picked it up. "Hi Matt, where are you? Dinner's all ready." A woman's voice answered, asking her if she wanted to do a survey on TV comedy shows. Melanie said no, and hung up in disgust.

It was 6:50 and Melanie was becoming more agitated by the minute. Matt hadn't been drinking for a couple of months, and had vowed he would never touch a drop again. Melanie had believed him, and planned this dinner as a rededication of their relationship. She couldn't imagine him breaking that vow, especially on their anniversary. He'd been diligent about attending AA meetings, although he never talked to her about them. Could he have thrown all that hard work away, and gone off on a binge again? Melanie's disappointment turned to anger, and she felt her heart beat faster as adrenalin shot through her. She decided to give Matt half an hour. If he wasn't home by then, it would be all over between them.

The doorbell rang. Melanie smiled and sang out in relief, "Come in Matt, the door's open." But her face fell as Rhonda, her neighbor came in, holding an empty measuring cup. "Can I borrow some milk?

3

I'm making biscuits and don't have quite enough." Rhonda saw the look of disappointment on Melanie's face and went over to her. "Oh oh, is this a bad time?"

"No. It's just that—I thought you were Matt. He often rings the bell instead of fishing for his keys. Come on in the kitchen. I'll get the milk."

Rhonda peeked into the dining room. "Wow, the table looks beautiful. You really went all out for him tonight, didn't you?"

Melanie nodded. "He promised to be home by six. He knew this dinner was a celebration of his sobriety, as well as our anniversary. The dinner is ruined, and I'm so angry and frustrated, I could scream."

Rhonda hugged her friend. "I'm so sorry. The last time Matt and I talked, he was adamant about not ever drinking again. I really thought he meant it. He said he knew that if he didn't quit, you'd break up with him. He must really be hooked on that stuff. Hey, I've got to go, my oven's on. Maybe he'll still show up."

Melanie poured some milk into the cup and walked Rhonda to the door. "I hope you're right, otherwise, he's out of here—for good!" She rearranged the flowers on the sideboard, and refolded the afghan on the sofa, tucking the pillows around it to make a soft place for Hero.

The grandfather clock chimed, signaling 7:30. Melanie threw up her hands. "Damn, he's done it again." She blew out the candles and shut off the music. She tried to tear the anniversary card in two, but was only able to rip part of the envelope. She scrunched the whole thing into a ball and tossed it in the trash. She was furious with Matt, and even angrier at herself for being taken in again. "Well, this is the last time. I'm going to ask him to leave, and I'm going to stick to it this time."

Melanie made a plate for herself, but was too upset to enjoy anything. She picked at the salad with little appetite, then cleared the dishes and put the food in the refrigerator. She sat down on the sofa. Hero jumped onto her lap and climbed up to her shoulder. Melanie hugged him, and rubbed her cheek on his soft fur. His "meow-meow" told her he understood how upset she was, and that he was ready to offer any comfort she needed.

At 8:15 Matt burst in the door and lurched into the living room, reeking of liquor and smoke. He went over to Melanie waving one pink and one blue-wrapped cigar, and said in a slurred voice, "I'm so sorry

I'm late. Eddie's wife had twins. We went to a bar to shelebrate." Hero stopped purring and his ears laid back. He jumped off Melanie's lap and made a beeline for the bedroom. Matt belched. "Ooopsh, I think maybe I had a few too many." He put his hand over his mouth and ran for the bathroom.

Melanie went into the bedroom and calmly took down Matt's suitcase. She put it, and his robe and pajamas on the sofa-bed in the guest room. She went back to her bedroom and locked the door, determined to kick him out in the morning. She didn't have the heart to do it tonight. He was too drunk to be out and about, although a night in the brink might do him some good. She was too tired and angry to confront him now, and knew she'd say things she'd' regret later. The suitcase in the guest room would be enough of a message for Matt. He'd spent many nights there when he'd come home too drunk to stand up.

Part I

Chapter 1
Melanie – One Year Later

Melanie looked at her image in the mirror at Nordstrom's. She ran her fingers through her hair to restore the strawberry curls that went astray when she was trying on clothes. "I like this suit," she said out loud, "but the color doesn't work with my red hair." Melanie took off the pink jacket and put on the dark green one. "That's better. This one's almost the color of my eyes, and it's perfect for the upcoming conference." She looked at the price tag and frowned. "A little pricey, but I love it. I'm going to buy it." She paid the clerk, waved at the pianist on the mezzanine, and headed for the front door.

Melanie's spirits were high as she started out, thinking about her meeting with Matt. She remembered the good times they'd had, how well he danced, and how much they laughed when they were together. She'd dated a couple of men she'd met through her massage therapy business, but neither of them were as much fun to be with as Matt. She'd stopped seeing them when things threatened to get too serious.

When she got to the farmer's market, the clock tower said 6:15. Matt's Mercedes wasn't in the parking lot. Melanie wondered if he'd traded it again. She was out of touch because they'd been apart for a year. She'd been surprised when he'd called last week. He said he had something to discuss with her, and she agreed to meet him here. Melanie suggested they cook dinner at her apartment so they could talk. Matt sounded sober, and she hoped he'd finally kicked the drinking problem that caused their breakup. Although she had a busy life, she'd been thinking about him lately.

Melanie shifted her purse and the shopping bag to her left hand, and tucked her briefcase under her arm. She loved the farmers' market. Their produce was fresh, and you could always find something new or unusual. She strolled down the aisles, glancing at tables piled high with fruit and vegetables. The after-work crowd thickened and jostled for a place at the booths, anxious to grab something for dinner and still make the early train home. Melanie spotted some flowers. She still had a little cash left after her shopping spree. Feeling extravagant, she headed toward the stand. The flowers were marked down. She chose the prettiest bouquet, and counted out $10.50 from her wallet.

Looking back toward the parking lot, Melanie saw a blond curly head bobbing above the cars. Slinging her purse over her shoulder, she grabbed her briefcase and shopping bag in one hand. Cradling the flowers in the other, she danced off. "Matt—Matt," she called, waving madly," but stopped short when she saw the curls were attached to a young woman pushing a baby carriage. Melanie sighed and her face fell. She thought about her friend Izzy, relaxing on the beach in Laguna, sipping a delicious drink with an umbrella and a skewer of pineapple in it. "I should have listened to her," she said out loud. "I could have been lying on the sand, enjoying the sun, instead of playing the same old waiting game with Matt."

The clock tower said a quarter to seven. Melanie began to seriously doubt that Matt was coming. She tried to block out the memories of when they were together, when he would call and cancel at the last minute, or just not show up. An argument always followed when he finally came home with a giant hangover, remorseful and apologetic. She remembered their last night together when Matt ruined their anniversary dinner by coming home after eight, drunk and obnoxious. Melanie sauntered back through the market, trying to put those memories out of her mind. The sun was half hidden by the buildings, but her blouse clung to her in the heat. Her right shoe was rubbing a blister, and she wished she'd changed to tennies.

Another half hour passed and the crowd started to thin, Vendors scurried to close their stands, putting leftover fruit and vegetables into packages, and marking discount prices on the plastic bags. Melanie was getting hungry and decided to buy some things for dinner. There was a seafood vendor in a shaded stand, but Matt was a meat and potatoes guy, so it was best to wait and pick up some steaks later. She bought some lettuce, a bunch of spinach, and a basket of cherry tomatoes. A ruddy clerk in a green apron bustled around and found a paper bag for the produce. A sign by the Armenian cucumbers said fifty cents each. Melanie found forty cents in her wallet. Fishing around on the bottom of her purse, she found a dime and added the cucumber to the bag. Juggling her packages, she headed back to the parking lot.

Twenty minutes went by. There were just a few cars left in the lot, and still no sign of Matt. She was hot and tired, her feet hurt, and her back ached. She dropped everything in the dust in the middle of the nearly-deserted farmers' market. Melanie knew there was a possibility that Matt might not show up, and was determined not to let it bother her. But in spite of all the self talk she'd done, she felt anger bubbling up inside of her. A few more minutes passed, and she finally accepted that Matt wasn't going to come. "This is it," she said vehemently. "He's out of my life. I'm going to call Izzy and see if her room has double beds."

Melanie pulled out her cell phone, but was distracted by a ruckus in the parking lot. An argument between two men accelerated to a scuffle, then into a full-fledged fistfight. A short scruffy man landed a punch to the chin of his opponent, who pulled a knife. He went after the other man shouting "Come back here you chicken bastard." The short man turned and ran through the parking lot, straight toward Melanie. The other man caught up with him and stabbed him on the arm, drawing blood. The two men raced through the market. One of them slammed into Melanie, hitting her cell phone out of her hand, and knocking her down. They continued their chase without looking back. Melanie landed on her knees in the dust, shocked and angry at this new bit of bad luck.

Several people gathered around and asked if Melanie was all right. She said she was, but inside she was seething, and on the verge of tears. She tried to get up and stumbled. A woman helped her get her balance. Melanie thanked her and looked around for her cell phone, but it was nowhere in sight. A bystander said he'd seen it fly out of her hand and land in one of the trashcans. She went to where he was pointing, and saw the tip of the phone sticking out of one of the cans. When she picked it up, her hand dipped into something wet and slimy. She pulled the cell phone out of a paper bowl full of stinky fish chowder. The phone had cracked in the fall. The soup had clogged the speaker, and Melanie knew it was a goner. A tear started, followed by a deluge. She put her briefcase on the ground and sat down on it. As she looked in her purse for a tissue, a shadow fell over her from behind, and a man came around and stood in front of her, blocking what was left of the day's sun.

Chapter 2 – Dwayne

Melanie looked up and saw a tall, handsome man in a cowboy hat looking down at her. He was wearing a blue denim shirt, jeans, and western pointy-toed boots. His blue eyes were striking against his tanned face. The man took off his hat and brought it to his chest. Bowing courteously he said, "Howdy Ma'am. Are you Melanie Parks?"

"Yes, and who are you?"

"My name's Dwayne Hathaway. I'm a friend of Matt Walters. He sent me to give you a message. He said I'd find you here." The man extended his hand. Melanie put hers out to shake it, then remembered the fish slime and wiped it on the tissue instead.

"Sorry about that." She picked up the demised phone and wrapped it in the tissue. "There's a long story about this. But tell me, is Matt all right? We were supposed to meet here at 6:00."

Dwayne frowned. "Matt won't be able to make it after all. He asked me to meet you instead. Can I give you a lift somewhere? You look all in."

Melanie looked at Dwayne. Although he was a complete stranger, he had an honest face and pleasant manner, and he said he was a friend of Matt's. Melanie decided it was okay to trust him, and gratefully accepted his offer. She stood up and brushed the dirt from her knees. "I'd love a ride home. These shoes are killing me. I'm going to carry them." She kicked off her shoes and picked them up, along with her briefcase and purse.

Dwayne had already tucked the packages and flowers under each arm. He guided her to a shiny blue Ford pick-up. The license plate said "Bar None." He opened the passenger door and helped her in, then put the bags and flowers in the back of the cab. Melanie heard a siren. She looked out the window and saw a squad car pull into the parking lot. She was still pretty shaken, and was glad that someone had called the police about the men that were fighting. Dwayne got in the truck and started the motor. Melanie turned the air conditioning vent toward her face, and the whoosh of cool air was a welcome relief. "What was Matt's message?" she asked. "Is he in town? Will he meet me later?"

Dwayne glanced at Melanie, noting that she was as pretty as Matt had described. He also saw that she was still very upset, and was trying not to cry. "It's a story I'd like to tell over dinner if you'll allow me. It's been a long day and I'm starved. Hey, I'd like to hear how the phone got slimed too. I'll bet that's a better story than any of mine."

Melanie made a face. "It's a doozer all right."

Dwayne looked around for a restaurant. "Could you eat something?"

Melanie stomach growled the answer and they both laughed. "There's a barbeque place about a mile from here that's pretty good, but I'd better pass. I spent every penny I brought waiting for Matt, and all I have is my Nordstrom's credit card with me. I just realized I couldn't make a call with this drippy phone when you showed up. I'd appreciate a ride back to my apartment though. It's just a couple of miles from here. You can tell me about Matt on the way."

Dwayne handed Melanie a bag with the remains of his fast food breakfast. "Why don't you stash the phone in here. It's kind of stinky. I'd be happy to take you home, but that's not going to get either of us fed. Would you let me treat you? I'd be mighty obliged." Dwayne turned to her. His boyish pleading look was hard to resist, and Melanie accepted his invitation.

They pulled into Birdie's Bar-B-Q and found a table in the back. The waitress took their orders, and Melanie headed to the bathroom to wash off the fish odor and refresh her face and hair. She tried to shake the anger she felt towards Matt, at least until she heard what Dwayne had to say. She straightened her shoulders and tried to smile as she returned to the table. The waitress brought glasses of iced tea. They quickly finished them and ordered refills. "Okay," Dwayne said, his eyes squinting up in the corners, "tell me where you got that recipe for cell phone chowder."

Melanie related the series of events, ending with Dwayne showing up just in time to find her holding the drenched phone. "They didn't even stop to see if I was hurt! I hope the police give them a hard time. She managed a smile. It's kind of funny now, but it sure wasn't when it happened. So tell me about Matt. Where is he?"

Dwayne looked closely at Melanie. "He saw that she had cheered up a little, and was hesitant to break her mood with his bad news. He took a deep breath and asked, "How much do you know about Matt? Have you known him long? Has he told you much about himself?"

Melanie was quiet for moment. Here she was being treated to dinner by a perfect stranger, and he was asking her all these questions. She took a long look at Dwayne. Sensing that he was sincere, she decided to plunge in. "I met him at a party. We were together for a while. At first things were great between us. Then a friend of mine got married. At the wedding, they poured champagne to toast the bride and groom. Matt drank his, than poured another. He ended up at the bar and got very drunk. I had to drive us home. It was funny because, before that, Matt always refused alcohol. He said he didn't like the taste. After that night, he started drinking heavily. We fought about it all the time. I kept asking him to quit, but he wouldn't. I finally said he'd have to stop drinking or leave. I gave him the address of an AA meeting. He stopped drinking for a couple of months, and said he was going to the meetings, so I planned a special dinner on our anniversary. Matt promised to be home on time. Everything was perfect, and I'd made all of his favorites. It got later and later, and I knew he was out drinking again. He finally came home, soused and sick. The dinner was ruined, and I was livid. The next day I asked him to leave. He said he was going to stay with a friend in New York."

Dwayne frowned. "Wow, that's tough. Have you seen him since then?"

"We stayed in touch, and spoke on the phone occasionally. After a time, I stopped hearing from him. I figured he'd met someone else. Then he called last week and said he wanted to see me. He sounded like the old Matt, happy and confident, and joking around. He made me laugh, like in the old days, so I agreed to meet him today. Then we were disconnected. I knew it was possible he wouldn't show up, but I hoped he would, and that he'd be sober. Is he in some kind of trouble?"

15

Dwayne shook his head. "I don't know. He called this morning and asked me to meet you here. I was at U.C. Davis, so I wasn't too far away. He was calling from a noisy place, a bar maybe. Someone kept interrupting, saying something like, 'Come on dude, we gotta go. This is our last chance to pull it off.' It sounded like there was some kind of scuffle, than a clattering like the phone had dropped. The background noise continued, but Matt had left the line. After a few minutes, the phone went dead."

Melanie sipped the last of her iced tea. "Wow, that's strange. I wonder why he sent you, and what kept him from coming himself. How do you know Matt?"

"We were buddies in high school. Then I was best man at his wedding."

Melanie looked up in surprise. She could feel a knot forming in her stomach. "Wedding! Matt's not married!"

"His wife died a few years ago in a car accident on Christmas Eve. Elizabeth wanted to go to services, and Matt said he'd watch the children. She picked up her mother and father. On the way back, a drunk driver ran a red light and crashed into the driver's side. Elizabeth and her father were killed instantly. Her mother was in a coma for a while, than she died too. Matt's children are being raised by his parents in New York. His father had polio and it's hard for him to get around, even with a cane. But his mother is a trouper. She takes care of her husband and the kids, and keeps a part-time job. They're both fine people."

"Married—and children! I wonder why he never told me any of this. Before he started drinking, we'd talked many times about spending our lives together. He never mentioned he'd been married before. We had discussed children, and Matt always said he didn't want any. Now it turns out he already has two." Melanie's resolve to remain unemotional dissolved. She lifted her head and, trying to hold back her tears, asked Dwayne to drive her home.

Dwayne paid the check and helped Melanie into the truck. She sat slumped over in the seat as she directed Dwayne to her apartment. He brought her packages inside, and put the flowers in the sink, turning the faucet on to wet the stems. When he came back into the room, Melanie was sitting on the sofa looking downcast. Dwayne was concerned, and didn't want to leave her alone. He sat next to her and put his arm around her. Melanie put her head on his shoulder and cried. She finally broke away saying, "You know, I just can't believe Matt had two children he never told me about." Seeing a wet spot on Dwayne's shirt she said, "Sorry, I've cried all over you."

"Don't worry about that, it'll dry." Dwayne grabbed a tissue and handed it to her. "Can I get you anything, a glass of water or coffee? Do you want to call a friend or relative? I don't think you should be alone."

"There's no one to call right now. My parents died when I was seventeen. Sara and Paula, my business associates, are away tonight. Rhonda, my neighbor, is at her daughter's, and my friend Izzy is spending a week at the beach. I was going to go with her, but when Matt called, I cancelled. I sure wish I'd gone with Izzy." Tears threatened to start again, but she forced them back as her practical side took over. "Craig Benson is the name of the person he was going to visit, but that was about a year ago. Say Dwayne, the things you heard in the background when you were talking to Matt sounded ominous, like they were planning to rob a bank or something. Should we call the police? Maybe Matt's in trouble."

Dwayne stood up. "I know. I was concerned too, but I didn't know where he was, or how to get him back." Dwayne looked at his watch. "It's a quarter of ten. I'll tell you what. We're both exhausted. I think we should sleep on it, than decide what to do in the morning. Is there a motel or hotel nearby? I'm all in, and it's a long drive back. I need to call the ranch too, and let them know where I am."

Melanie thought for a moment, than, throwing caution to the wind said, "Why don't you spend the night here? I have a guestroom in back with a comfortable sofa-bed. You can make your phone call while I scare up some blankets. We can talk more over breakfast. Tomorrow's Saturday. Do you have to get back for anything?"

Dwayne looked relieved. "I'm much obliged for the offer. I could sleep for a week, and don't relish trying to find a room at this hour. I don't need to be back as long as they know I'm okay, but I don't want to put you to any trouble. I promise to be a perfect gentleman. And—I know to put the toilet seat down." His grin was most endearing.

Melanie laughed. "I would have guessed that of you. Come on in the back. I'll show you the digs and make up the bed."

The smell of fresh coffee and the sound of bacon sizzling on a grill awakened Dwayne the next morning. The sun was already high in the sky. It had been a long time since he'd slept in. Even on weekends there was work to do at the ranch. By seven, everyone was sitting around the breakfast table planning the day. Melanie had left a shirt on the dresser that looked about his size. He found a new toothbrush and razor alongside the fresh towels Melanie had left in the bathroom. An unopened bar of soap and small bottle of shampoo on the counter said "Marriott" on the label.

Dwayne showered and shaved, put on the shirt and his jeans, grabbed his hat, and went to find Melanie. She was talking on her cell phone. "I know. What a shock. Married, and two kids—and drugs, can you imagine!" Melanie listened for a minute. "Yeah, Izzy, he's a real cowboy. He stayed overnight. No, Dwayne's all right. He's been a perfect gentleman. If I find out anything else, I'll call you. I'm glad you're having fun. I wish I'd gone with you. Okay, bye."

Melanie turned to Dwayne. "Sorry. I didn't mean to label you. Good morning. Did you sleep well? I made some breakfast."

Dwayne laughed and pointed to his boots with his hat. "Hey, it fits." He noticed how pretty Melanie was in a green summer dress that accentuated the soft curves of her figure, and matched her eyes. Her hair was still damp from the shower. Reddish-blond curls clung in tendrils around her face. Tantalizing odors wafted up from the frying pan. Two glasses of freshly-squeezed orange juice sat on the counter, and coffee dripped steadily into a carafe. Dwayne tossed his hat on a chair "Mmm, it sure smells good in here. Thanks for the duds. The shirt fits fine, and mine definitely needs a tub of suds. You look like you're doing much better this morning. Did you get some sleep?"

Melanie retrieved two English muffins from the toaster and buttered them. "I tossed and turned until after midnight, then finally dozed off. I had a terrible dream—but never mind that. The shirt's Matt's. He left some things here, hoping we'd eventually get back together. Would you like some orange juice or coffee?"

"Both please, and a sample of whatever you're stirring up over there. It smells wonderful, and I'm hungry as a bear."

Melanie dished up plates of eggs scrambled with onions and peppers. She added the crisp bacon and muffins, and brought the coffee and two mugs to the table. Dwayne spread strawberry jam on his muffin. "Mmm, this is good. I'll have to Tell Luz about putting peppers in the eggs." They ate quietly for a few minutes, than Melanie broke the silence.

"I'm still mad at Matt for all the things he's done, and all the lies he's told me, but I'm also concerned about him. I've been thinking about calling the police, but there's nothing for them to go on. Matt's not really missing. He may have called from a cell phone, and they disconnect all the time. And he did call you to come and get me. The scuffle you heard on the phone could have been some of his buddies roughhousing. Plus, we don't have a clue where he called from. It could have been a bar, or maybe a party. If we reported what happened, I don't think the police would think we had any case at all."

Dwayne nodded agreement. "The police won't even go looking for a person until he's been missing more than 24 hours, and Matt isn't really missing. But there's something about the whole business that bothers me. Oh, by the way, Craig Benson is the children's godfather. I never quite figured him out. He always looked like he needed a good night's sleep and a shave, and he always flashed around a lot of money. He drove a brand new BMW, and spent money lavishly on women and booze. I always thought it was odd they chose him for the children's godfather, but he really loved those kids. He spoiled them, and brought them expensive presents when he visited. I lost track of Craig after Matt's wife died. Do you know him?"

"I never met him, but Matt spoke of him often. He said Craig was a good friend, but he was always trying to talk him into doing something he didn't want to do. He never said what it was. Matt also seemed to always have plenty of money. He traded his Mercedes every year. I still can't believe he has two children. He never said one word about them. How old are they?"

"Let's see. Susan is six, and Julie must be four now. I haven't seen them for a long time. They're really sweet little girls."

Melanie shook her head. "Okay, enough about Matt. Whatever's going on with him, there isn't a thing either one of us can do about it, at least not right now. So tell me about you."

Chapter 3 – The Ranch

Dwayne grinned. "Me? I'm a confirmed cowboy and I love it. My family owns a ranch up north, near Sonoma. It's called the Bar None Dude Ranch. We live in the main house, and rent the cabins to vacationers—mostly families who want their children to see what it's like to live on a working ranch. We give riding lessons, and teach the kids how to milk a cow, saddle a horse, and hoe a straight row. There's a big dining room in the main house where the guests eat breakfast and dinner. Our staff is like one big family. Most of them have been with us for years. They run the house and ranch like clockwork. I supervise the ranch, and Dad takes care of the business end. We hold classes in woodworking for the guests, and most of the furniture in the cabins was made in the woodshop. Every morning Jenny and I ride around the place and look at everything. I give an order here or there, but most of the time the job's already been started. We have hoedowns and barbeques in the evening, or sit around the campfire and tell ghost stories. Scares the little ones to death, but they love it. Most families come back year after year."

Dwayne's blue eyes sparkled with pleasure as he talked about the ranch. Melanie started to see him as a person for the first time. He was very attractive, in a rugged kind of way. His dark hair shaded to gray at the temples, and his blue eyes lit up with enthusiasm as he told his story. He was lanky and fit. His hands were big and strong, and he seemed thoroughly happy with himself and his life. Listening to him talk, Melanie felt a twinge of jealousy. How she wished her own life was so neatly packaged up and tied with a bow. "So that explains the cowboy duds. But what's a hoedown?"

"Whoa, little lady—you haven't lived until you've been to a hoedown at the Bar None Dude Ranch. The staff tosses their aprons when supper's over. They put on western shirts and cowboy hats and become the Bar None Country Band. They play everything from fiddles to harmonicas. We square dance and do some line dances. When everyone's about worn out, the music turns to country blues. Luz, our cook, has a beautiful voice. She croons the rest of the evening away, and we dance 'till we drop. There's nothing like it. We have hoedowns a couple of times a month, and Dad teaches square dancing on the weekends."

Melanie sighed. "It sounds wonderful. I'd like to see it some time."

Dwayne stood up excitedly. "Hey, when's your next vacation?"

"This is it. I took the next two weeks off to go with Izzy to the beach, then when Matt called…"

"Say, why don't you drive up with me and spend some time at the ranch? There are plenty of rooms in the main house. Or, if one's free, you could stay in one of the cabins. Come on, it'll do you good to get away for a while. I guarantee you'll have a good time."

Melanie's face lit up. "I'd love to. When Matt didn't show up, I was thinking about joining Izzy at the beach, but the ranch sounds like it would be more fun. How much does it cost though? It sounds like it's for rich people who own horses and expensive cars."

"Not at all. Anyway, you can go as my guest. And don't worry, you'll earn your keep." Dwayne's eyes sparkled mischievously and Melanie screwed up her face. "Naw, kidding aside, I see you're a great cook. You can help with dinner if you want to. And there are lots of other chores the guests pitch in and help with. It's all in good fun, and we'll let you take a break now and then."

Melanie laughed, but wasn't quite convinced. "It sounds great, and I'm tempted, but what if Matt changes his mind and comes by?"

He can reach you on your cell phone." Remembering the slimed phone, Dwayne grimaced. "Sorry about that."

"Actually the demised phone is from work. I'll have to replace it. I have another one I can take, but I don't have a thing to wear. Everything I own screams **city.** I'll stick out like a green thumb, or whatever you cowpokes call us."

Dwayne laughed. "Greenhorn, but don't you worry. All you need is a pair of jeans and a tee-shirt and you'll look like you spent your life on a ranch. Come on, Melanie, it'll be fun, and it'll get your mind off things. I'll take you home when you've had enough. Please say you'll come." The boyish look appeared again, and Melanie melted and agreed to go with him to the ranch for a couple of days. She started to bring the dishes to the sink, but Dwayne put his hands up. "No you don't, lady, I'll do that. You did the cooking. Besides you have some packing to do. Bring a sweatshirt and jacket, and a bathing suit. The stream's cold, but the pool's heated. The hot tub feels great in the evening if you have enough courage to brave the cold night air." Dwayne bristled with energy and whistled "Country Roads" as he cleared the breakfast dishes.

Melanie disappeared into the bedroom to see what would be suitable for a week at a ranch. She suddenly burst back into the kitchen. "Wait a minute. What about Jenny? What will she think about your bringing a perfect stranger to the ranch?"

Dwayne threw his head back and laughed. "Jenny'd like it fine. She's my horse. She takes to all of our guests."

Melanie giggled. "Do I feel silly. I thought she was your wife!"

Dwayne shut the water off. She could see his grin fade as sadness clouded his face. "Cindy died a year ago. She had breast cancer. When they found it, it had already spread clear through her body. The doctors tried everything, but nothing helped. After a while, she decided she'd rather live her last days in comfort. She stopped all treatment, and lived on morphine until the good Lord took her. I know she's better off in heaven than suffering here on earth. But I'm danged if I can understand why such a good woman had to go through all that."

It was Melanie's turn to comfort Dwayne, and she went over and put her hand on his arm. "I'm so sorry." Dwayne drew her to him and held her close. She could feel the muscles ripple on his back as he struggled to control his emotions. She finally broke away and asked, "Do you have children?"

"We wanted them, but Cindy never conceived. After they found the cancer, the doctors figured one of the tumors prevented her from getting pregnant. We were married for four years, and they were happy ones. Cindy loved the ranch. She taught the children to ride, sang like a meadowlark, and played a great game of tennis." Dwayne sighed.

"Hey, I didn't mean to get you down. You have enough to chew on already. It's over now, and most days I'm able to put it behind me and not think about it."

Melanie's eyes glistened, but she struggled to put on a happy face. "Then it's all settled. I'll finish packing, then it's off to the Bar None."

It was just past eleven when they stowed the last of Melanie's things in the truck. Dwayne started the motor and went a few feet, then stopped. "Say, do you play tennis? There's a court at the ranch. When enough of the guests are players, we do a challenge tournament. If you want to play, bring your racket along."

Melanie nodded and her eyes sparkled. "I love to play. I'll get my things." She went back inside and put her tennis outfit and hat in her bag, along with a wristband, headband, and a new can of balls. She checked to make sure she had her favorite racket, than brought everything back to the truck, and they were on their way.

Dwayne opened a CD case. He had a selection of music ranging from country western to jazz. "What would you like to listen to?" Melanie chose a Carly Simon CD and they sang along to the Itsy Bitsy Spider medley.

They stopped for lunch at a diner, walked around for a while to stretch their legs, than got back on the road. The lack of sleep caught up with Melanie. She dozed off in the comfortable cab. Her head lolled to the left, and it was soon was resting lightly on Dwayne's shoulder. He let her sleep, remembering the dream that disturbed her the night before. The warmth of her body and light scent of her hair tantalized him. He had not dated since Cindy died, and he'd forgotten how nice it was to be so close to an attractive woman. At 3:30, he pulled into a gas station. Melanie woke up and stretched. "Oh my gosh, I went out like a light. Are we there?"

"We're about an hour and a half away. We should be getting in just before supper time. I called ahead, so they're expecting us. I'm going to gas up and get a coke. Do you want anything?"

"A coke sounds good. I'm going to freshen up and browse around the store to stretch my legs. I'll meet you back at the truck in ten."

Chapter 4 – More Surprises

They drove for a while in silence, than Melanie turned to Dwayne. "You know, there are still some pieces missing about Matt. For one, why are his parents raising his children? Matt seemed to have plenty of money, and many single fathers raise their kids."

"Hoo boy. I was afraid you'd open that can of worms. Well, here goes. When his wife died, Matt went off the deep end. He started drinking heavily and got into some pretty heavy drugs. Then he got involved in some stock deals that went bad. He had a bad temper when he drank. He hit someone, and was arrested for assault. Craig bailed him out of jail. Craig tried to get him to go to AA, but Matt wouldn't go. His parents tried to get him to shape up and pay attention to his family. When they saw it was hopeless, they took the children. Matt didn't fight them, he seemed to have given up on life. At first he visited his kids regularly, but his parents were always pushing him to stop drinking. He saw them less and less as the years went by."

Melanie sighed. "So when I met him he was sober, but when he drank the champagne at the wedding, the disease took hold again. It's all beginning to make sense now. Was Matt coming back to patch things up with me, or was there some other reason?"

"Well the truth is, Matt said when he first called you he had every intention of trying to get back together. Then he realized he couldn't hold it together with you for very long. He decided it was best to make a clean break. He was going to tell you it was over for good, then for some reason, he lost his nerve. He asked me to meet you instead and give you the message. I told him I didn't think that was such a good idea, but before he had a chance to answer, his buddies interrupted and the phone went dead. I'm sorry I didn't tell you this yesterday, but you were so upset, I thought you'd already heard as much as you could handle."

There was a long silence as Melanie digested this last bit of information. "It's funny. I know I should be sad, but instead I'm relieved. It's clear now that Matt was a whole other person than the one I thought I knew. He kept his entire past from me, including that he'd been married, had two children who he stopped seeing, and had a history of drugs and alcoholism. And jail! I don't know how he kept all that from me, but somehow he had me completely bamboozled. I realize now that I'm better off without him." In spite of her words, tears sprang to her eyes, but she wiped them away resolutely. "You know what? I'm not going to think about Matt for two whole weeks. I'm on vacation, and I'm going to enjoy it."

Dwayne patted her hand. "Smart girl." A few minutes later they saw a road sign that said Forest Lane. Dwayne turned right onto a well-maintained gravel road. "Here we are. Welcome to the Bar None Dude Ranch." He swung another right, and drove under a big wooden sign with a Bar and a Zero etched on it. Dwayne pushed a button, and a big iron gate opened to a long narrow road. About a quarter of a mile in, Melanie could see a cornfield on the left, and apple and pear orchards on the right. They passed a hot tub and swimming pool. A tennis court peeked out from behind the bathhouse. The road curved to the right revealing an enormous vegetable garden completely surrounded by wire fencing. Everything looked lush and green. Some people were dismounting their horses and walking them toward the stable. To the left, Melanie could see a fenced area where sheep nibbled away at the grass.

Dwayne steered the truck up the hill toward a big white ranch house. A couple sat on the porch playing checkers, and a young boy swung from an old tire hanging from an aging oak tree. A woman snipped roses from the bushes that bordered the porch. An older man in overalls pulled weeds from a flower garden. Dwayne parked the truck and jumped out, then helped Melanie down. "Hi Dad," he said, and gave his father a bear hug. "Thanks for holding down the fort. Dad this is Melanie Parks. She's a friend of Matt Walters. She's here as my guest for a week or two. Melanie, this is my father, Tom Hathaway."

Tom wiped his hand on his overalls and shook Melanie's hand warmly. "Well we're mighty happy to have you. I hope your stay will be comfortable, and if we have anything to do with it, it'll be fun too."

"Are any of the cabins available?" Dwayne asked. "If not, Melanie can stay in the east wing."

"As a matter of fact, the Silverman's just cancelled. Donny's got the chickenpox, bless his heart. Jane's afraid the whole kit and kaboodle are going to get it. I told them to stay away from here until they're poxless. They had reserved the cabin out by the pond."

"That's too bad about Donny. I'll set Melanie up in nine then. How are Mom and Aunt Jody? Gosh it seems like I've been away for ages!"

"Jody's as feisty as ever. Your mom says she's okay, but I can see that her leg's still giving her trouble. I think if she'd keep off it for a spell, it'd heal. But you know your Mother, you can't tell her anything." Tom threw up his hands in exasperation. "God knows I love that woman, but she can be as stubborn as an old mule when it comes to taking care of herself. We've got some other news though. Anabelle's carrying twins. The vet said we should keep an eye on her and call him when its time. It's likely to be a hard delivery."

"Hah, I knew it. Anabelle's our prize cow. She's almost ready to deliver, and she's enormous. She looks like she's going to have an elephant. Wait 'til you see her. She's the prettiest thing, and she's gentle as a lamb. Her big brown eyes could melt a candle." Dwayne handed Tom a bottle of huge capsules. "These are from the vet at U.C. Davis. He said to give her two a day until she delivers."

Melanie laughed. It was the first time she'd heard a cow being referred to as pretty. "Twins! I didn't know cows could have more than one at a time. I can't wait to see her."

Tom nodded. "We were surprised too. It happens mostly in crossbreeding studies when the cows are given hormones that cause multiple ovulation. If the calves are both heifers, one or both will be sterile, so we're hoping for one of each gender. Twin calves' weights are likely to be lower than normal. If both births are successful, the mother may only want to take care of one calf. We'll have to watch closely to make sure they both get enough milk."

Dwayne nodded. "You can be sure they'll get plenty of attention from the folks around here. Anabelle's everyone's favorite. Come on

26

inside and meet the others, then we'll get you checked in and bring your things over to the cabin." Dwayne held the screen door open, and they went back through the house to the dining room. "Hi Mom, I brought a new guest." Dwayne hugged his mother. This is Melanie Parks, a friend of Matt Walters. Melanie will be staying in nine for a couple of weeks. Melanie, this is my mother, Ida."

"Well a big welcome to you. That cabin's all ready 'cause we were expecting the Silvermans, but Donny got the chickenpox." Trying not to favor her leg, Ida came around the table and held her hand out to Melanie. "You'll like it out there. The ducklings are especially cute this year, and the frogs'll put you to sleep in no time. Goldie's off with the kids somewhere. They'll bring her in when dinner's ready. Goldie's our golden retriever. She's full grown now, but we still think of her as a puppy because she's so playful. She can wear you out in no time, pulling on a rope, or chasing after a tennis ball."

Dwayne led Melanie into the kitchen. Melanie, this is Luz, chief cook and crooner. She runs the galley during the day and sings up a storm at night. This is her husband, Marcus. He's always there when you need him. Hilda heads up the crew in the house. Look out for her, she's Ms. Perfection," he teased.

Hilda laughed and turned to Melanie. "We're glad to meet you. Now you be sure and let us know if there's anything you need."

Ida took the key for cabin nine off its hook and handed it to Dwayne. "Go ahead and get Melanie settled in, then come on back for supper."

"Let's take the truck. The cabin's quite a ways back. If we drive over and drop off your things, we'll still have a few minutes to look around before dinner." They got back into the truck, and drove down a one-lane road that ran through a wooded area behind the ranch house. Log cabins peeked out between the pines. Here and there a patch of mountain ferns shared space with scatterings of blue lupine and wild morning glories. Bright orange California poppies occupied the sunniest spots. "Look," cried Melanie. "There's a deer, and another! They're so graceful."

"There are plenty of them around here, and they're voracious eaters. They'd eat everything you plant if you let 'em. That's why we put the fence around the vegetable garden. We purposely put the roses up against the front porch where there's always someone to shoo them away. They've learned not to come around the house, at least during the daytime, but they still do some damage at night. Last year they nibbled Mom's prize floribunda down to the nub. Boy I've never seen her so mad. Take care not to get too close though, or try to feed them. Although they look tame, they're really wild creatures. They can deliver a lethal kick if they feel threatened. A couple of years ago, Tommy tried to pet an especially tame one he'd named Bambi. The doe came tearing down the hill and went after him. You've never seen anyone run so fast."

"Who's Tommy?" Melanie asked.

"He's a child we fostered for a while. We were hoping we could adopt him. His parents had gotten into some trouble with drugs, but they shaped up and were able to get Tommy back. They're all doing well now and we still see them every once in a while. Here's the cabin." Dwayne unlocked the door and Melanie saw with surprise that, what looked on the outside like a plain woodsy log cabin, was a beautiful cozy cottage on the inside. It was furnished country style with carved oak furniture. There was a kitchen with an oak table and chairs. A vase of flowers graced the table, and a bowl of fresh fruit sat on the counter. Chintz curtains hung from the windows. Wood was piled high in the fireplace, and another stack lay on the hearth.

Dwayne carried Melanie's suitcases into one of the bedrooms. He put them on a big four-poster bed that was covered with a beautiful hand-made quilt. "Mom made that. She can't just sit and do nothing, so she keeps busy making quilts when her other work is done. The bathroom's small, but there's a shower and tub." Dwayne opened the door revealing an old fashioned claw-foot bathtub.

Melanie clasped her hands together in delight. "Oh, it's wonderful. I never dreamed—I mean, I always thought a ranch would be meager somehow."

Dwayne grinned. "We're pretty civilized here. We aim to keep our guests coming back, and we want them to tell other folks good things about us. Keeps us on our toes, but we wouldn't want it any other way. Come on out back and see the pond. The frogs make a racket during mating season, but it's a nice sound." The pond was surrounded by a grassy meadow. A small deck held a redwood table and chairs, and a swing hung from a tall tree. As Melanie took everything in, a blue jay flew down and scolded them for invading his territory without bringing a peanut. "Its perfect—paradise on earth. Thank you for bringing me here." Melanie flew into Dwayne's arms and hugged him.

"Whoa. Oh, that's nice. I'm glad you like it, and it's good to see you smiling." Dwayne held her a minute, then reluctantly let her go. "Guess we'd better get back to the house. They'll be waiting dinner for us."

Melanie stepped back and caught the look of pleased surprise on Dwayne's face. "I'm sorry," she cried. "I didn't mean to be so forward." A tinge of pink flushed her cheeks, and her hands flew to her face. "It's just that, well, my vacation started out so awful and it's turning out so nice." Dwayne's heart skipped a beat. He felt something he hadn't for a long time, and knew he'd done the right thing by inviting her here.

On the way back, they saw families walking up the hill toward the ranch house. Children bounced around and joked and teased each other. Goldie bounded in and out trying to greet everyone at once, licking any hands she could reach. When she saw Dwayne, she made a beeline for the truck. She jumped excitedly at the open window until he stopped the truck and scratched her silky ears.

The dinner bell sounded, and everyone's steps quickened. Soon the house had swallowed up all the guests. Each took a place at the long tables laden with food. Platters were piled high with fried chicken, mashed potatoes, salad and corn on the cob. Dwayne parked the truck, and he and Melanie joined the others. When all were seated, Tom folded his hands and said a simple grace, thanking the Lord for good friends, good food, and a bountiful harvest. Then everyone dug in and started talking at once.

Dwayne introduced Melanie to the others. "Jody, this is Melanie Parks. Melanie will be here for a week or two. I'm sure you two will get a chance to talk later. This is Aunt Jody, Dad's sister," he said, turning to the elderly woman on his left."

"We're so glad to have you. Please call me Jody, everyone does. I'm too young to be called aunt, and much too feisty." She frowned but her eyes twinkled.

"So you say Jody, so you say" laughed Dwayne. "Don't believe her. The truth is, Jody acts like she's fierce, but underneath she's as soft as down. She sees everything that goes on here, and understands it better than anyone. There's not a one of us that could get through a crisis without a talk with Jody, and we all come away the better for it."

Chapter 5 – Ida

Ida looked across the table. "Now, where's that salad dressing Luz just made? It's very good." Ida pushed her chair back and tried to stand up, but her leg buckled, and she grasped the table to keep from falling. Dwayne jumped up and helped her back into the chair.

Tom scowled. "Looks like its time to go see Doc Elmer. Long overdue too. This thing's gone on way too long."

Melanie looked concerned. "What happened? Were you in an accident?"

Ida made a face. "Naw. They're making too much of it. It's just my old sciatica acting up again. Only thing is, most years it comes and goes. This year, it started hurting the beginning of spring, and it just keeps on hurting. I figure the best treatment is to ignore it."

"Maybe I can help. I'm a nurse, and I also do massage therapy. I specialize in treating soft tissue injuries. I'd be happy to look at it. I'll be able to tell right away if I can relieve the pain, or if it needs to be looked at by a doctor."

"Bless you child. Would you? I'd be most obliged. It does get hard to ignore when it interferes with my activities. Where do you work?"

"I do nursing during the day at a hospital, and also share a massage studio with two other therapists. One specializes in acupressure, and the other does shiatsu massage. We find that many injuries respond best to all three treatments, and we cross refer our clients. It's a great set up. We all practice each type of treatment so we can cover for each other when one is away. We have a pretty good success rate, but every so often we refer a client to a doctor or chiropractor if their injury is more than we can handle. Sara and Paula are covering for me for the next two weeks while I'm on vacation." Melanie turned to include everyone at the table. "By the way, I want to tell all of you how much I'm enjoying myself. Thanks for your warm welcome, and for making me feel so comfortable." She turned to Dwayne. "And thank you for bringing me here. I'm already having a good time."

"It's a pleasure to have you, and it looks like you won't have to do kitchen duty after all." Dwayne teased. "There are more aches and pains here than you can count. When the others find out what you can do, they'll be lined up clear out to the pond. But Mom's first. If you can do something for her leg, we'd all be grateful."

Luz came in with a luscious looking tunnel-of-fudge ring cake. The fudge frosting dripped into the center, and everyone oohed and aahed as she cut slices. After dinner, the men retired to the front porch. The women gathered around Melanie asking questions about her work, and how she'd met Dwayne. Luz and the band freshened up, and went out on the back deck to set up their instruments.

Dwayne extracted Melanie from the women who had surrounded her. "Would you like to go for a walk while it's still light?"

"Sounds great," she replied, patting her stomach, "but I haven't eaten that much since Thanksgiving. I don't know if I can move, let alone walk. Everything was delicious. Jody and your parents are great. They're so warm, and seem to care so much about each other. You're lucky to have such a nice family."

"I know. I wouldn't trade them for anything." He led Melanie toward the barn. A group of children were milling around chattering excitedly. One of them started jumping up and down and gesturing for them to come. "Hurry," he shouted, "I think Tiger's having her kittens."

Dwayne and Melanie ran to the barn just in time to see the first born wriggle out onto the hay. Tiger chewed the cord, than vigorously licked the kitten until it began to mew. Dwayne drew one of the children aside. "Go get Aunt Jody. Tell her to bring the birthing kit. She always knows what to do if it's a hard delivery. Tell her it's Tiger, not Anabelle." The next kitten was already well on its way when Jody arrived with the rest of the family. Dwayne filled her in. "Looks like everything's okay, but I wanted you to be here just in case."

Jody kneeled down next to Tiger. "I'm glad you called me," She turned to the others. "This is going to be Tiger's last litter. She's past her prime, and as soon as these kittens are weaned, it's off to the vet with her. It's high time she retired from motherhood."

Melanie edged toward the front. She saw a beautiful tiger-striped cat with huge yellow eyes and a long furry tail. The cat was enormous. Everyone watched as five kittens of various colors were delivered, cleaned, and tucked under Tiger's ample belly. Melanie loved cats. She missed Hero, her beloved Calico that she had to put to sleep last year. Hero became diabetic when he was eighteen years old. He had to be tested for sugar in his blood, and Melanie gave him insulin shots twice a day. When they'd exhausted all efforts to keep him comfortable, Melanie agreed with the vet that it was time to let him go. She held him and stroked him during the injection, and cried when the cat closed its eyes and drew its last breath. It was the saddest thing she'd ever had to do. She'd thought about getting another kitten, but never had time to follow through.

Tiger suddenly stopped licking her brood and shook the kittens off her. Labor began again, and she looked like she was in distress. Jody knelt down and touched Tiger's belly. She felt several hard contractions. After a few minutes, Tiger let out a yeowl and expelled an orange and white kitten, bigger than the others. It wasn't breathing. Jody scooped it up and wrapped it in a towel. She cleared mucus from its mouth, and massaged it until the kitten started to breathe normally. She placed it next to Tiger, who licked it clean and helped it find a nipple. Everyone let out a collective sigh of relief, and the children's' eyes were wide with awe as they saw the kitten they thought was dead, jockeying for a place next to the others.

They watched for a little while, than Jody got up. "Okay kids, time to go." No one moved. The children were overwhelmed by the miracle they'd witnessed, and they wanted to stay to make sure the orange kitten was all right. "She'll be okay. The mucus was preventing her from getting air, but she's perfectly fine now. From her size, I suspect she'll end up the leader of the litter. The kittens need to sleep now, and Tiger can use some rest too. We'll check on them tomorrow morning. Now no sneaking back to the barn tonight," she warned them. "You all need your rest too. Promise?"

"We promise Jody," they echoed, and took off in different directions to tell their families the news.

The strains of the fiddlers could be heard from the barn. Dwayne and Melanie started back. "Do you want to dance a while?"

Melanie shivered in her light dress. "I think I'll pass tonight. I'm really tired—and it's getting cold. I should have brought my jacket."

Dwayne threw his jacket around her shoulders, and guided her down the road toward her cabin. "There's never a dull moment around here, but that was more excitement than even I bargained for. Tell you what, there's a bottle of wine in the fridge in your cabin. Let's drink a toast to the two weeks ahead. Then I'll let you get some sleep."

Melanie sighed. "That sounds good."

Soft lights on the cabin doors lit the path as they walked down to cabin nine. Melanie unpacked while Dwayne opened the wine and poured two glasses. He handed one to Melanie. "Here's to some really good times."

Melanie raised her wine glass. "And to a great new friend." She yawned and stretched. "I'm going to turn in early. I need to catch up on some sleep."

"Breakfast's at seven and chapel's at eight if you want to join us. Can I call for you at six so we can take a walk before breakfast?"

"Six o'clock on a Sunday morning? Have mercy! Oh, all right. Come and get me. I'm used to getting up early."

Dwayne reached out with both hands and drew Melanie to him, holding her in a hug that wasn't nearly as brotherly as before. They could hear each other's hearts racing, and neither wanted to let go of the moment. Finally Dwayne said, "I'll see you in the morning then." He planted a kiss on Melanie's forehead. "I'm really, really glad you came. See you tomorrow."

Chapter 6 - A Scare

After Dwayne left, Melanie sat for a while thinking about him. She liked his style, and his hug had felt nice. She daydreamed about how it would be to kiss him. She knew it would feel very good. She let herself imagine that they were holding each other and kissing. A warm feeling crept through her, and she knew it wasn't just from the wine. The good feelings lingered while she unpacked her things and soaked in the tub. She called Izzy on her cell phone, but got her answering machine. She left a message for her to call back, then climbed into her pajamas, burrowed under the thick quilt, and fell into a deep sleep. She dreamed again, this time of Matt walking backwards away from her, and Dwayne coming towards her with his arms opened wide. He was about to kiss her when she woke up with a start.

The lighted travel clock said 2:15. It was quiet, and very dark. Melanie wondered what had awakened her. Then she heard a noise just outside the window, and sat straight up in bed. Fear crept through her body. A few minutes passed. Melanie finally started to relax, then froze again as she heard a rustling near the window, and something scratching on the pane. She jumped out of bed, turned on the light, and grabbed her robe. The scratching stopped, and she heard something running away from the cabin. For a moment, she couldn't move. She listened intently, but all was quiet again.

Melanie felt goose bumps rise on her back and arms. Several minutes went by, but it stayed quiet. She suddenly came to her senses. "It must have been a deer," she said out loud. She turned off the light and crawled back under the covers, but it was close to four when she finally dozed off. She dreamed of Matt again. This time he was coming toward her with an ominous look on his face, and Dwayne was nowhere

in sight. She slept fitfully until morning. When Dwayne knocked on
the cabin door at six, Melanie awakened with a start and sat straight
up in bed. Remembering last night's happenings, she called out "Who
is it?"

"It's me, Dwayne."

Melanie sighed in relief. "Just a minute." She grabbed her bathrobe,
and unlocked the door. "Boy, am I glad to see you. I had a visitor in
the middle of the night that scared me to death. Something scratched
on the window. When I turned on the light, I heard it run away, but
I couldn't get back to sleep for a long time. I don't know why I'm so
jumpy. Come on in, I'll put some clothes on. I'll just be a sec." She
took some jeans and a shirt out of the dresser, and disappeared into
the bathroom.

Dwayne went outside and looked around. There were smudge
marks on the window, but the thick layer of pine needles on the ground
prevented him from making out any prints. He came back inside just
as Melanie came out of the bathroom. "Something was here all right. It
smudged up the window. It could have been a deer. I'm sorry you were
disturbed. I know how much you needed to sleep."

Melanie sighed. "I told you I was a greenhorn. It's so quiet here
at night. At home you wouldn't hear a little scratch on the window. It
would be masked by the sound of freeway traffic. But hey, I'll get used
to it." She grabbed her jacket. "Come on, let's go for that walk. I want
to see everything." They locked the cabin, and Dwayne led her back
to the barn to check on the kittens. Each had latched onto a nipple
and was contentedly kneading Tiger's belly. The orange kitten suckled
alongside the others, showing no further signs of distress. Dwayne
refilled Tiger's food and water dishes. Melanie petted her soft head.
"Good job, Tiger. You're a good mom." They walked over to Anabelle's
pen where they had isolated her until the twins were born. Melanie'd
had no previous experience with cows. "Can I pet her?"

"Sure," Dwayne said. "Feel her ears, they're soft as down."

Melanie had never been up close to a cow, and she tentatively put
out her hand. Anabelle looked up at her trustingly, and shifted her
forelegs to get a better footing. Melanie stepped back. "She certainly is
huge. Is she due soon?"

"In a week or two," Matt wrapped two of the capsules in grass
and fed them to Annabelle. "Good girl," he said as he patted her head.

"Come and see Jenny, she's in the stable." Each horse had its own stall with a fresh layer of straw on the floor, some water, and a feed bin. Dwayne greeted the horses by name, and gave each of them a piece of apple. "This is Jenny," he said, stopping at a beautiful rust-colored horse with a white face and neck. "Hey girl. I brought you a visitor. Bet you thought I'd forgotten about you. Don't worry, we'll go riding later today." The horse whinnied and nuzzled Dwayne's hand, looking for the treat. Dwayne turned to Melanie. "Do you want to go riding with me this afternoon?"

Melanie petted Jenny's mane. "I'd embarrass myself. I'm so out of practice. I haven't ridden a horse since I was a kid."

"It'll come back," Dwayne promised. "It's just like riding a bike. Once you know how, you never forget. We have a couple of really gentle horses, like Danny here." He moved to the next stall, and patted the brown and white Paint on the head. "Danny'll break you in easy." They looked at a couple of his other favorites, than Dwayne glanced at his watch. "Its time we headed back to breakfast. I don't know about you, but I've worked up an appetite again."

Back at the house, the talk was all about the kittens. The children almost bounced out of their chairs in anticipation of seeing them again. They chattered incessantly about which one they were going to bring home. Finally Ida put her hands up. "Whoa now. All the kittens have been spoken for. Everyone wants Tiger's kittens, and they put their claims in way ahead of time. The disappointed children let out a chorus of 'awes.' Sorry about that kids. But I did check them early this morning. They're doing fine, even the orange one. Tiger needs to rest now, and the little ones need to nurse. After chapel we'll take you up to see them, but no touching yet." Quiet was restored and they tore into the pancakes, eggs, and bacon.

Chapter 7 – Diagnosis

After breakfast, the family and many of the guests walked up the hill to the chapel where Tom presided over a short non-denominational service. Afterwards, Melanie asked Ida if she still wanted her to look at her leg.

"I sure do. Let's go back to the house and find a place where we can have some privacy." They went into the bedroom, and Ida kicked off her shoes and stretched out on the bed. Melanie examined her foot, than moved her hands up to her ankle, and her leg. "Tell me if I'm causing any pain."

Ida was quiet until Melanie pressed right above her knee, then she jumped. "That's the sore spot—right there." The area was red and slightly swollen. She tested Ida's range of motion on both legs, than asked her to turn onto her stomach. She applied pressure to several areas on the back of her legs, and on her upper and lower back and neck, but Ida reported no further discomfort. "What do you think? Can your massage therapy help me?"

Melanie looked concerned. "I'm afraid not. What you're experiencing isn't presenting like sciatica. Usually the sciatic nerve causes pain in the foot, calf, and lower back as well as the leg. But your pain seems to be concentrated in your leg, just above the knee. You need to see a doctor to find out what's going on."

Ida's face fell. "You don't think it's anything serious?"

"It could be, or it could be absolutely nothing. Really, it's best that you get a doctor's opinion. I'm not qualified to diagnose this type of thing. They'll probably want to get an x-ray and do some blood work."

"Drat. I hate all that stuff," Ida fussed. "I guess I'd better tell the others. I'll call Doc Elmer and make an appointment for next week."

Melanie turned away so Ida couldn't see the concern on her face. "Better make it for tomorrow. The sooner you get it diagnosed and treated, the sooner you'll be back on your feet. Meanwhile, it would be best if you kept off your feet, and elevated your leg as much as possible."

"Okay, whatever you say," Ida sighed, dreading what was coming.

Melanie went to find Dwayne. The house was deserted. Figuring everyone was up at the barn, she grabbed her jacket and started up the road. Dwayne met her halfway, full of questions. "How's Mom? Is it anything you can help with?" Melanie's face set off an alarm. Dwayne took her arm. "Oh oh, what is it?"

"I don't think its sciatica." Melanie explained about the pain being isolated in one area. "The redness and swelling indicate a blood clot. Does Ida have a history of heart disease?"

"Not that I know of, but Mom is so stubborn, she hasn't been to a doctor in years. She hates taking pills, and won't take an aspirin if she can help it. A blood clot! That's serious. Is she in any danger?"

"Yes, she could be if it isn't treated. If the clot breaks off and travels to her lungs, it could cause a lot of trouble. I didn't tell Ida what I suspected. That's up to you or Tom. I told her she should see a doctor right away. Meanwhile she should keep off her feet, and elevate that leg as much as possible."

Dwayne sighed. "She's been complaining for years, and none of us thought to force her to see a doctor. You've probably saved her life Melanie. I'm much obliged."

"You know, she probably did have sciatica before, but the symptoms she presents with now are very different than those she described having before. So don't blame yourself. It's good we caught it now though, so she can be treated."

Dwayne shook his head. "I need to tell Dad. Will you come with me and tell him what you suspect?"

Melanie nodded. They found Tom talking to a ranch hand in the corral. Dwayne waited until they were through, than motioned his father to come over. When Melanie told Tom what she had found, she saw his face fall. "It could be a blood clot, or it may be nothing, but it should be looked at by a doctor as soon as possible. Meanwhile she needs to stay off her feet. I didn't tell Ida how serious it could be. Do you want to tell her, or wait until she sees the doctor?"

Tom thought for a moment. "Let's wait until tomorrow. If Doc Elmer can't see her right away, we'll tell her and get her into emergency. If it's something serious, I think Ida would do best getting the news from the doctor. I'll fix her up in the recliner and spend the day paying bills so I can keep an eye on her." Tom turned to Melanie and put his hand on her arm. "God bless you for finding it. I don't know what I would have done if something had happened to Ida. I'm thinking the good Lord must have brought you here on purpose." He gave her a hug, then walked dejectedly back toward the house.

Dwayne took Melanie's hand. "Let's pick some flowers and give them to Mom with strict orders to sit all day and do nothing. Darn, I know that's the one thing that's hardest for her to do." They found a basket and clippers in the garden shed, and Dwayne unchained the wire gate. She followed him along the path to the cutting garden behind the vegetables. Some pumpkin vines had crept through the fence in a corner of the garden. The leaves were huge, and the vines sprawled far and wide, winding into the field beyond the garden. There were only a few pumpkins on each vine, but they were already huge. "How did you get such big ones?" she asked Dwayne.

"I beg your pardon." Melanie saw the blush on Dwayne's face, and laughed as she pointed to the pumpkins.

Dwayne laughed. "Ah, the pumpkinus giganticus. Now that took some work. First we chose a variety that produces big pumpkins. Then we only let one or two grow on each vine. When the blossoms set, we selected one or two female blossoms and cut off all the others."

Melanie grinned. "You cut off the male blossoms? How do you tell a female blossom from a male?"

"The female has a slight swelling beneath the flower that's a potential pumpkin. You tear the petals off a male blossom, and fertilize the female by softly rubbing pollen on the inside of the female blossom. That starts the baby pumpkin growing. If you want a really big one, when they're about the size of a melon, you select the biggest to nurture. Then you cut off all the others. That diverts all the plant's energy to the pumpkin that's left."

They looked at each other and Melanie went cross eyed. "Well, thanks for the lesson in plant husbandry."

Dwayne made a face. "Hey, you asked." Their smirks turned to giggles, and they sat on the bench and laughed until tears came. Some of the stresses of the day dissolved with their laughter, and they returned to the house feeling much better. Hilda had prepared a comfortable place for Ida on the recliner in front of the TV. Her sewing box and quilt pieces were close by. A cup of tea and some fresh-baked muffins sat on the table next to her. Goldie sat watch, sensing instinctively that her presence was needed. Tom sat at the old roll-top desk, sorting the bills into piles. Dwayne handed Ida the bouquet. "Here are some flowers from the garden. I heard the news. Now I'm not going to say I told you so, but you should have gone to the doctor as soon as this thing started."

"Hush now," Ida said. "I feel bad enough, and have scolded myself already, so the rest of you don't have to add to it."

Melanie looked at the set up. She suggested adding a pillow to raise Ida's legs slightly higher than her hips. "That'll take the pressure off the leg a little. It's also a good idea to get up and walk around every ten or fifteen minutes to keep your circulation going."

Hilda took the flowers into the kitchen and brought them back artfully arranged in a pewter vase. "These are beautiful. The delphiniums are so pretty with the pink carnations and white daisies."

Dwayne kissed his mother. "I see you're being well taken care of. Hilda, do you need anything from town? If not, we're going to go riding down by the stream."

Hilda called the question in to Luz, who popped her head out of the kitchen. "We've got everything we need here. You two go and have a good time. Do you want box lunches? I'm making some for the guests."

"That'd be great. He looked at Melanie. I'm going to borrow Sharon's hat for you. You can't go riding without a proper hat." He grabbed a hat off the rack in the hall and placed it on Melanie's head, then tipped it at an angle. "Fits fine," he said. "Now you look like a real cowgirl."

Chapter 8 - Silver Creek

Luz produced the lunches and some bottled water, and Melanie and Dwayne took off for the stables. The horses seemed to know they were in for a run. They waited impatiently until their saddles and bridles were in place. Melanie looked at Danny with trepidation. "Gosh, I don't remember horses being so tall. Can you give me a boost?"

"Sure, let me help." Dwayne brought a mounting block for Melanie to step up on. He guided her foot into the stirrup and helped her into the saddle, than walked around and placed her foot in the other stirrup. He adjusted the leather straps and handed her the reins. "Okay. Ride-em cowgirl."

Melanie looked down. "Yikes, it's so high up here. Maybe I should start with a pony."

"Don't worry, you won't fall off. We'll start off slow. We're going to Silver Creek, my favorite place on the ranch." Dwayne mounted Jenny and set the pace. Danny followed, sensing he was carrying a beginner. They walked the horses around the ranch until Melanie found her seat. Dwayne pointed out the corral and orchards, and stopped to speak to several of the hands.

"Wow, its all coming back, just like you said. I remember having a great time riding when I was a kid." They found the dirt road that led to the creek. Dwayne clicked to Jenny and she moved to a trot. Danny followed suit, and Melanie found herself bouncing up and down on the saddle. Youch, she thought. Then Jenny broke into a rocking gallop, with Danny close behind her. The whistling wind took Melanie's breath away, and trees flew by on either side. After several miles, the landscape greened up and the trees grew closer together. Soon the road began to narrow. Dwayne pulled on the reins, and Jenny slowed to a walk. Danny followed without a signal from Melanie, and she began to appreciate how well trained the horse was.

They could hear the tinkle of water before they saw the stream, meandering lazily over gravel and rocks, and disappearing around a bend. Hundreds of birds inhabited the trees. Each sang its own song, resulting in the sweetest chorus Melanie had ever heard. One suddenly flew off, and the others followed with a cacophony of flapping wings. She saw flashes of red as they took flight. "Oh, they're beautiful, what are they?"

"Red-winged blackbirds. We have lots of them around here. They stay mostly near the stream. Some wild blackberry bushes are growing a little farther downstream. If the birds haven't already picked them clean, we're in for a treat." They traveled downstream for another quarter of a mile. "There it is, my favorite spot." Melanie looked where Dwayne was pointing and saw a sandy beach with big flat rocks on the left shore. A little further upstream, blackberry bushes sprawled onto the bank. They dismounted and tied the horses close enough to the water so they could drink from the stream. Dwayne took the lunches and water bottles out of the knapsack. They took off their shoes and socks and waded in the shallow stream. The weather had warmed up, and it felt good to splash in the cool water.

They left the lunches on a rock, and went over to the blackberries. "Watch those thorns," warned Dwayne. "They can be vicious, but the berries are so good, it's well worth the trouble. They're sweetest when they're dark black, but still shiny. In the spring we pick buckets full. Luz makes them into blackberry pie and jam. I'm afraid the only ones the birds haven't eaten are way inside, so be careful." They poked through the brambles and plucked all the ripe berries they could reach, eating them as fast as they picked. "Ouch," Melanie cried out. "You're right about the thorns. They're wicked, but the berries are yummy."

They finally stepped back. In spite of all the berries they'd eaten, they were still hungry. "Let's see what Luz packed." They devoured the sandwiches in the lunchboxes, than tucked the remains back in the saddlebags. They continued downstream, picking a berry here and there for dessert. Around the bend they saw a sandy beach and sat down. They buried their toes and fingers in the warm sand, and enjoyed the hot sun on their heads.

Melanie lay back and stretched her arms over her head. "Mmm, this is the life. I could stay here forever, but right now I could sure stand a nap. I don't know if I'll ever catch up on my sleep."

Dwayne nodded. "The fresh air does that to you. It happens to everyone when they first come to the ranch. You'll get used to it after a while. By the end of the week you'll be able to go all day and sleep like a baby at night."

"That would be nice. Say Dwayne, Do you really think it was a deer that scratched on the window last night? Could it have been a bear, or a mountain lion?"

"We're not high enough for bears, but there have been some puma sightings at some of the campsites near us. It could have been coyotes too. They sometimes come down from the hills to catch a tasty snack."

Melanie shivered, and Dwayne saw the look of concern on her face. "Would you be more comfortable moving into the main house? There's plenty of room, and we often put guests up there. I live on the west end. In the east wing, there's a private studio we added when my sister and her husband were living with us. It has a bedroom and sitting room, a private bathroom, and a little kitchen. It has its own entrance and deck. The suite is attached to the house, but can be locked off for privacy. You know, come to think of it, with Mom sick, it might be comforting having a nurse up at the main house."

"It sounds inviting, but I hate to be so much trouble. I think I'll stay in the cabin one more night, than I'll decide."

Dwayne leaned over Melanie. "Okay, but the more I think about your moving up to the house, the better it sounds. I'd like having you closer. I know I shouldn't say this. We've only known each other for a short time, but I'm beginning to care a lot about you. It kind of scares me, and at the same time excites me, and brings back feelings I haven't felt for a long time." Dwayne brushed a curl away from Melanie's face. He kissed her on the forehead, then lightly on the lips. She put her arms around him and kissed him back. Melanie's lips tasted like the sweet berries. Dwayne held her close, thinking he never wanted to let her go. Then Matt's face came to his mind, and he broke away. "Are you and Matt still—I mean, do you still have feelings for him?"

Melanie sat up. "I've thought about that a lot since our talk. You know, I've come to realize there was no such person as the Matt I thought I knew. He was just a figment of my imagination. When we broke up, I went through the process of getting over him. I only agreed to meet him because he sounded sober on the phone, and was joking around like the old Matt. But after what you told me, the lies and drugs, and neglecting his children, it's clear that we were never meant to be. I have only compassion left for him. Any love that was there is gone. How about you, do you still think a lot about your wife?"

Dwayne shook his head. "When Cindy died I cried for weeks. Jody really helped. She has some straightforward, no-nonsense ideas about life and death that helped me to understand that, just because Cindy was gone, that didn't mean my life was over. It took a long time, but I finally started participating in ranch activities and enjoying life again. Until I told you about her the other day, I hadn't thought about Cindy for a long time. I'll always keep her memory tucked into a corner of my heart, but there's a big part of me that's still empty. Since I met you, I've been feeling the need to fill the rest of that space. I know Cindy would have wanted that person to be someone special, someone like you."

Dwayne stood up. He took Melanie's hands and pulled her to her feet, then took her in his arms. Melanie relaxed against him, and her arms crept around his neck. He kissed her softly, and she returned his kiss. Melanie finally drew away. "Yum, that feels even better than I dreamed it would." Melanie realized she'd given herself away, and a slight blush crept up her cheeks.

"So you've been dreaming of us kissing, huh. Well, I have to admit I did some thinking about that too." Dwayne kissed her again. "Mmm, it's much better in real life.

They held each other close until Melanie finally broke away. "We'd better get back."

Dwayne kissed her again. You're right. We need to see how Mom's doing. Hey—there's square dance lessons tonight. Do you want to take a stab at it?"

"I've never tried, but if I can ride a horse, I can learn to square dance. Do I need a full skirt and a crinkly petticoat?"

"Naw, we're pretty casual here, even at hoedowns. Tonight's for beginners. Dad shows the newcomers the basic steps, and teaches a simple dance that's easy to learn. It's really fun." They walked back to the horses. Dwayne showed Melanie how to place Danny next to a rock so she could mount him on her own. They were both lost in their own thoughts as they rode back to the ranch.

Part II

Chapter 9 – Scat

Melanie and Dwayne turned the horses over to Lance, the stable hand. Back at the house, everyone had gathered around Ida. A box of chocolates sat on the table, and more flowers adorned the buffet. Ida's eyes sparkled. "I haven't had this much fun in a long time. I should've played sick long ago," she chuckled. "I'm going to be right spoiled."

Dwayne laughed. "Enjoy it, Mom, you deserve some rest, and you'll be back on your feet soon enough. I'm glad to see you're having a good time. We're going down to Melanie's cabin so she can get changed. We'll be back for dinner."

As they strolled lazily toward the cabin, Dwayne whistled *The Itsy Bitsy Spider,* and Melanie hummed along. "Catchy, isn't it? Speaking of spiders, we have some whoppers here. Some species are beautiful, and they spin incredible webs that are perfectly symmetrical. We'll try to find one tomorrow." Melanie unlocked the cabin and went inside. Dwayne walked around the back to take a look. Melanie showered, and put on clean jeans and a perky lightweight blouse. Remembering the chilly evenings, she grabbed her jacket and went to look for Dwayne. She found him in the woods across the meadow. He was kneeling and looking at something on the ground. Melanie called out and he started back, carrying something in his handkerchief.

"Looks like your visitor was a coyote. I found scat, and it's got traces of blackberries in it." He showed the contents of the handkerchief to Melanie and she shuddered. "It must have had dinner at our spot by the creek before coming here. And look over there." He pointed to a scattering of yellow feathers by the pond. "Looks like the berries were just the appetizer. Roast duckling was the main course."

49

"Why the rotten . . ." Melanie exclaimed. How could it eat those cute little things?"

Dwayne pointed to some yellowish stains on the deck. "It looks like he's marked his territory as a warning for the others to stay away."

Dwayne saw Melanie's face go white. "That means—oh, my gosh—if I'd left the window open, I would have been dessert!"

"No, no." Dwayne's eyes twinkled. "Coyotes don't eat people. They're afraid of us. He was mighty interested in your smell though. That's why he was sniffing around the window. Believe me, if he'd seen you, he'd have taken off pronto."

"That's comforting. I think." But Melanie wasn't convinced. She looked around as if she wouldn't be surprised to see the whole pack coming out of the woods. "You know what, moving into the east wing is beginning to sound better and better."

"I'll tell you what. It's getting late, and we'll have to do some cleaning in there. Right now we need to get back for dinner. How about if I hang out on the sofa at the cabin tonight so you can get a good night's sleep?" He held up his right hand and his blue eyes crinkled at the corners. "Don't worry. I promise to be a good boy, although it'll be a heck of a lot harder this time than when I stayed overnight at your apartment."

Melanie laughed. "I don't know who to be more afraid of—you or the coyotes! Come on, I'll race you back," she said, getting a good head start. Dwayne pretended to let her win, then overtook her just as she reached the porch, and they ran laughing into the house. Their cheeks were red, and both were out of breath.

"Well, look at this. What have you two been up to? Dwayne, you look like the cat that swallered the canary." Jody grinned as she ushered them into the dining room. "There's a bit of pie and ice cream left, but the pork chops and gravy are all gone." She winked at Tom, just as Luz came out with two plates she'd saved for them. Melanie was ravenous, and couldn't remember anything ever tasting so good.

"A coyote was prowling around Melanie's cabin last night," Dwayne announced. "Almost scared her to death, scratching on the window. It left scat in the forest, sprayed a couple of places on the deck, and helped herself to one of the ducklings. Have you heard anything from the other guests?"

"No one reported anything." Tom said. "You know, that cabin is far away from the house, and it's too isolated. Melanie, you should move your things into the main house. There's plenty of room in the east wing. You'll feel safe here, and get a good night's sleep."

"I told her the same thing Dad. We'll move her things in first thing in the morning. I'll spend the night on the sofa at the cabin tonight to make sure Melanie's safe." Jody saw Ida's raised eyebrow as she pretended to concentrate on her pie. "I'll bring one of the pistols. If the coyote comes back, I'll blast a shot over her head to make her see the error of her ways."

Melanie stayed to help clear the dishes. When the fiddlers started warming up, the kitchen staff shooed her off to join the dancers on the deck. Tom was organizing the newcomers into couples, and forming squares. An experienced couple was assigned to each group. Dwayne took Melanie's hand and led her to one of the squares. Tom adjusted the microphone. "I want to welcome everyone to square dance 101. What we're going to learn tonight is real easy and just for fun. But if you turn left instead of right and end up in the square behind you, you're gonna get six swats with a wet noodle." Everyone laughed.

"Okay now—head couples raise your hand. Right, now the side couples. The person you're standing next to is your partner and the one behind you is your corner. These are your home places. We'll refer to these terms often, so do your homework and get 'em straight. The first call's easy. Join hands and circle to the left. Now swing your partner. Gents, that means take your girl in your arms and swing her once around. When you get back where you started, twirl her under your arm and place her back at your side. Now, swing your corner, than guide her back to her place next to her partner. Let's try it. Circle to the left and swing your partner. Good, now swing your corner." The dancers went every which way. The head couples untangled the mess and put everyone back in place in their squares again. Tom laughed. "Same thing happens with beginners every time. Don't worry, you'll catch on quick enough. All the ladies raise your hands and turn to your partner. Okay, gents raise your hands and turn to your corner. Got it? Okay. Let's learn something new."

"The next call is allemande left with your corner girl, do si do your own." The head couples demonstrated. "Okay, let's try it." Again the squares got hopelessly tangled but after several more tries, everyone had mastered the steps. "Okay folks, let's add the music. Everyone go to your starting places. Hey there, Joe, square up that square over in the corner. That's better."

Tom signaled the band and they played "Oh Johnny, Oh" as Tom called in a sing-song voice:

"All join hands and you circle the ring.
Stop where you are, give your honey a swing.
Swing that gal behind you—that's your corner.
Swing your own and, if you have time when you get back it's
allemande left with your corner girl.
Do si do your own.
Then you all promenade, with your sweet corner maid,
singing oh Johnny, oh Johnny, oh."

Everything went well until the promenade, than the squares fell apart. Almost everyone grabbed the wrong person, and some were left with no partner. "No fair," they shouted good-naturedly. "What's promenade? You never told us about that!" Tom laughed. "Okay. It's real simple. Turn to the gal behind you. That's your corner. No, no, the one right behind you." Gentlemen, cross your hands and hold on to hers. Now bring her around next to you and walk her around the square 'till you're back home. Now you have a new partner, hopefully the girl that used to be your corner. When you get home, twirl her out and place her by your side." After some practice, everyone had mastered the steps and were able to join Tom in the chorus…"Singing oh Johnny, oh Johnny oh."

Melanie's eyes shone. "This is great. I've done some country western, and love line dancing, but this is much more fun."

They went through the dance several times. Then Tom said, "Okey, dokey, time to close up shop. You did well, but remember, we're having a test next week so you'd better practice."

Dwayne and Melanie walked around to the front of the house and sat on the porch swing to catch their breath. Dwayne glanced at Melanie. She looked beautiful. Her eyes danced with excitement and her cheeks were flushed. She leaned back and put her hands behind her head. "This is such a great place. When I tell Izzy about it, she'll be green with envy. None of our vacations have ever been this much fun. I don't know how I can ever thank you."

Dwayne squeezed her hand. "Your being here is thanks enough. I'm going to get the gun and some blankets and pillows. I'll try to persuade the kitchen staff to part with another bottle of wine. Hey, try to sneak some of those chocolates. We can't let Mom eat 'em all."

A full moon lit up the path as they walked to the cabin. "Hoo boy," teased Dwayne. "Those coyotes will be a-howlin' tonight. A full moon makes 'em really hungry."

Melanie skipped ahead. "Get out of here. You're just trying to scare me. I know all about coyotes now, and I'm not scared of them any more." Just then a squirrel ran across their path and scampered up a tree. Melanie jumped and grabbed Dwayne, dropping the pillow she was carrying.

Dwayne laughed as he dusted off the pillow. "Okay. You get this one tonight. I want the clean one."

Melanie grabbed the pillow back. "Oh no you don't, that one's mine." They teased and scuffled all the way to the cabin, then unlocked the door, turned on the lights, and dropped the bedclothes on the sofa.

Dwayne put the gun in the top dresser drawer, than turned to Melanie. "You know, you are the loveliest thing." He pulled her close, and wrapped his arms around her.

She sighed and snuggled into his shoulder. "I keep thinking this is a dream that will disappear when I wake up. You are such a dear man. I've never met anyone as nice as you, or as much fun." She stepped back, and the saucy look on her face suddenly turned serious. "You really **are** nice aren't you? You don't have any hidden flaws or dark secrets in **your** past do you? Melanie put her hands on her hips. "Dwayne Hathaway, if you aren't who you seem to be, please tell me now before I let myself get in too deep."

"I know how you must feel after what you went through with Matt. I'll tell you all about me. Let me know if you see any red flags. I'm probably a couple of years older than you. I snore if I roll onto my back in my sleep, and I tend to be a little too neat—leftover from my days in the army. I love the ranch, and wouldn't live anywhere else. I took a job as a programmer at Nextech after I graduated. I hated being inside all day, and gave notice after six months. I need to feel the sun on my head and the earth at my feet. I want to ride in the open space. That's who I really am. Is that someone you could learn to love?"

"Oh Dwayne, I'm already halfway there and it's scaring me to death." They reached for each other and their kiss started softly, than became more intense. Melanie stroked Dwayne's hair, and rubbed her hand against his cheek, then drew back. "Dwayne, I care about you very much, and I want you more than anything in the world, but I don't want to rush into anything."

"Me too, I've thought about nothing but you since you flew into my arms behind the cabin. But I agree we should take things slow. We've only known each other a short time, but you know Mel, this seems so right. I know that time will only make our feelings grow stronger."

Melanie thought for a moment. "What I would like for tonight is for us to stay in our clothes and just hold each other. It wouldn't feel right to make love, but I want to wake up in your arms. Would that be all right with you?"

"It's more than I'd hoped for, and it sounds exactly right. Come on, let's open that wine."

Dwayne was awakened at six by the alarm clock in his head that always went off at that time. He untangled himself from Melanie's arms and watched her for a minute. She stirred slightly, then relaxed and turned over and went back to sleep. Dwayne felt a sweet mixture of wanting and caring stirring inside him. He took a shower, and came out of the bathroom just as Melanie was waking up. She turned onto her back, stretched, and opened her eyes. When she saw Dwayne, she sat up on the edge of the bed and smiled at him, than looked down at her rumpled clothes. "Oh my gosh, look at me. I look like I just rolled out of bed!"

Dwayne laughed. "You did!"

Melanie patted the space next to her on the bed. "But you, you look wonderful. Mmm, you smell good too. Come here." Dwayne sat down next to her and put his arms around her. He kissed her, and Melanie licked his lips. "Yum, you taste good too." She got up and stretched, then gathered some things for her shower. "Were there any wild animal attacks last night? I didn't hear anything, but I was so tired I could have slept through an earthquake. Did you hear anything?"

"Not a thing, but I'll take a look around while you're in the shower." Dwayne came back to the cabin just as Melanie finished dressing. "Something was prowling around again last night. There are more feathers on the meadow, and more scat and markings. It looks like our coyote had another picnic. We're going to have to figure out how to scare it off before we let any other guests stay here. Let's pack up your things after breakfast and bring them back to the ranch house." Melanie nodded. This time she didn't need convincing. They put on their jackets and walked back to the main house. Luz and Marcus were bringing in platters of French toast, bowls of fresh fruit salad, and vanilla yogurt. Jody was telling the children that the kittens needed a couple more days to settle in before they could pick them up.

"Awe, we want to play with them."

Jody smiled. "I know, but we need to give them a little more time. Their job right now is to nurse, sleep, and keep warm so they can get nice and strong. Don't worry, they'll be running around and begging for attention soon enough."

The children sighed. "Okay. I guess we can wait a few more days. We'll just watch for now."

Chapter 10 – Dr. Elmer

Tom motioned Dwayne and Melanie aside. "Melanie, will you do the talking when I call Doc Elmer? You can explain things better, and answer any questions he might have." Melanie nodded. "Good. We'll make the call right after breakfast. His office opens at eight."

They joined everyone in the dining room. Melanie filled her plate and drizzled pure maple syrup over her French toast. "This looks so good. I'd better watch it or I'll be the size of Anabelle in no time!"

Dwayne choked, and said in a muffled voice he thought only Melanie could hear, "Are yours gonna be twins too?"

"Now you." she said, poking his arm. "Cut it out." They laughed, than realized everyone was looking at them.

Tom grinned. "Hey, it's good to see you two having fun." He peeked at Ida and saw that her eyebrow was raised even higher than before.

Dwayne sipped his coffee. "The coyote was back last night. It left more scat and got another duckling. We're going to have to figure out some way to scare it off before we put another guest in that cabin."

"Yup," Tom agreed. "We can't fence the whole area. Maybe a bunch of us should go into the woods and pee all over. Some folks say human urine repels coyotes and mountain lions. It hasn't been proven though. It's just a theory. I'll call 'round later and see if the ranger has any advice."

After breakfast, Tom, Dwayne and Melanie slipped away to call the doctor. Tom told the receptionist who was calling, and she put him right through. Dr. Elmer knew the Hathaways from way back. He'd taken care of Dwayne and Sharon after they were born. He'd nursed them through their childhood diseases, and set and casted Dwayne's broken arm when he fell out of a tree. Tom told the doctor about the pain Ida had been having. He explained that Melanie was a nurse and had examined her leg. Melanie took the phone. She told the doctor her findings, and what she suspected.

The doctor sounded concerned. "It sounds like a blood clot all right. She should have a complete work up right away. You did the right thing by saying she should come in today. You probably saved her from complications that could have been very serious. Put Tom back on and I'll tell him what to do to get things started."

Melanie handed the phone back to Tom. "I'm pretty sure Melanie's right about the blood clot. Ida needs to be seen right away. You should bring her to the emergency room as soon as you can. We'll admit her from there, and run some tests."

Tom felt a knot forming in his stomach as he digested the doctor's instructions. "Ida doesn't know Melanie suspected a blood clot. Should we tell her?"

"Well now, seeing its Ida, it's probably best not to say anything until the tests come back. I know how she feels about doctoring. No sense scaring her to death if it turns out to be nothing. By the way, I told Melanie it was real savvy of her to realize it was more than sciatica this time. I'm pretty sure the tests will prove that she was right about its being a blood clot. She probably saved Ida from having a lot of problems. If the clot had broken off and gone to her heart, she could have had a stroke. You are lucky folks to have such a good nurse at the ranch right now."

"We sure are. Thanks Doc. I'll get Ida ready and bring her in as soon as I can."

"Great. When you get to the hospital, have the desk call me and we'll get things started right away. And Tom, try not to worry. It sounds like Melanie caught it quick enough to treat, and worrying won't help a thing. See you later this morning then."

Tom put one arm around Dwayne and the other around Melanie and told them what the doctor said. "Doc's right about not worrying. It won't do any good, and we need to keep calm around Ida. No sense getting her riled and her blood pressure up."

Jody came in, wringing her hands and looking agitated. "Dwayne, I just remembered you had a call from that fella you went to school with. What's his name, Matt something? I swear I'm losing my mind.

I can't remember a thing any more. Anyway, it was a couple of hours after you called and said you were bringing Melanie here. He said he wanted to talk to you about something important. I told him you were on your way in, and were bringing a woman friend." Jody crossed her arms over her chest. "He sounded upset and kind of ornery—you know, like he used to get sometimes. Gosh, I'm sorry. Seems like more and more things slip my mind lately."

Dwayne put his arm around Jody. "Don't you give it a thought. With all that's going on around here, it's a wonder any of us remember anything. I'll give Matt a call later and see what he wanted. Right now we have something to tell you. Let's get the others in here too."

When they were all gathered around, Tom told them he'd talked to Dr. Elmer. "He's very concerned, Ida. He wants to see you in Emergency this morning. He wants to do some tests. Now don't start in worrying. We won't know anything for sure until we get the test results. Melanie, he said to tell you that was good detective work. We're all mighty appreciative."

Melanie smiled. "I'm glad I could help."

Ida frowned. She'd seen Melanie's concern when she'd examined her, and guessed something serious was going on. She just kept pushing it out of her mind, hoping it would go away by itself. "Okay, if there's no getting out of it, but I sure don't relish having to go to the hospital and deal with all that poking and stabbing and x-raying." She sighed and went off to put a few things in a bag.

Jody followed her. "Now Ida, you worry too much. Things are never as bad as you imagine. Doc Elmer will fix you up as good as new in no time, and the hospital isn't all that bad. When I had my appendix out, they treated me like a queen."

Ida hugged her sister-in-law. "Thanks Jody. It's just that I hate all that stuff, all the pills and shots, and bedpans." She sighed. Well, it looks like I'm going to have to go, so I may as well make the best of it."

Dwayne put his hand on his father's arm. "Dad, do you want me to come with you to the hospital?"

Tom thought for a minute. "Naw, we'll take the Chevy. She's gassed up. It's just an hour and a half to town, and we're not likely to know what's going on until tomorrow. I'll stay overnight at the Ellison's. You'd best stay here and take care of things. All the bills are paid, but it's the end of the season, and some of the guests are checking out this morning. They'll need some attention. Marcus, can you keep an eye on Annabelle?" Seeing the glum looks on everyone's face he said, "Listen folks, don't you worry. If the good Lord saw fit to send us this smart little lady who knows all about such things, then he certainly has some miracle in store for Ida. I can't see it any other way."

Melanie couldn't help but admire the way Tom handled things. He was firm, but compassionate. He loved to play, but was all business when the need was there. His faith was strong. He loved his family, and was ready to put them first whenever it was necessary. She'd already noticed Dwayne had many of the same qualities.

Tom called Sharon and brought her up to date on Ida, including a description of Dwayne's new friend who'd diagnosed her. "She's a sharp cookie, and very pretty. I can see that they're fond of each other." He winked at Melanie and Dwayne.

"That's great. It's high time that Dwayne started dating again. Should I come up?"

"Don't come now. It'll just scare Ida. It's best to wait until we know what's going on. Doc said the tests will be back late tomorrow. How's Jeff?"

Sharon sighed. "He's okay, I guess. He's been putting in a lot of overtime, and sometimes doesn't get home until late. We're both well though. Call me as soon as you know something. Hugs to you all, I love you."

Dwayne brought his cell phone into the east wing and dialed Matt's number. He was transferred to an answering machine and left a message.

Melanie tried not to show how rattled she was about Matt's call. She struggled to keep a pleasant face and say the right things, but Dwayne could tell she was upset. She took her cell phone to a quiet corner and punched in Izzy's number. She got her answering machine, and left a message. "Hi Izzy, I'm not home. I'm at the Bar None Dude Ranch. I came up here with a friend of Matt's. Call me back when you get a chance." That'll give her something to think about, she thought, than laughed as she pictured the reaction Izzy would have. She called her office. "Hi Sara, how are things going? Are you getting along okay without me?"

"Girlfriend, it's good to hear from you," Sara wailed. "Aren't you smart to take this week off. We're swamped. Hey, there's something going on at the hospital. I heard there were budget cuts and some layoffs."

"Wouldn't you know it. I take a couple of days off, and everything falls apart. Hey, guess what. I'm spending some time at a dude ranch with a friend of Matt's. He's a real sweetheart. I'll tell you all about it when I get back. I'm going to call the hospital and find out what's going on. Meanwhile, don't work too hard." Melanie called the Hospital. "Scheduling please," she said. Her call was transferred to Lilly Carter. "Hello, this is Melanie Parks. I'm on vacation, and I'll be back in two weeks. Can you look on the books and tell me when I'm scheduled to work."

Lilly put Melanie on hold for a minute, then returned and said, "You're not on this month's schedule at all. That budget cut they've been talking about went through. Many of the nurses have been laid off."

"Wow! Okay, thanks Lilly." Melanie hung up and sat down to think. What bad news! Or was it? Maybe it wasn't so bad after all. It might be a good way to disconnect from a job that was stressful and time consuming. It would give her time to expand her business, or explore other things—like Dwayne Hathaway—who she was finding more and more charismatic. Is it possible that this was meant to be? Now I'm sounding like Tom, she thought, and went to find Dwayne.

He was sitting on the porch swing holding his cell phone and looking gloomy. "I couldn't get Matt so I left a message. Say Melanie, do you think he changed his mind again and wants you back?"

Melanie shook her head. "I don't know. After what you told me about him, anything's possible. Don't worry though. Now that I know who he is, it's really over between us. I have some news too. I'm not scheduled to work for the rest of the month."

Dwayne jumped up. "That's great, that means you can stay longer." He grabbed her around the waist and swung her around, then twirled her out until she was breathless. They sat down again and he asked, "Say, could you have been laid off too?"

"I have a lot of seniority, but it's possible. I know I should be worried, but right now I just don't care. I'm beginning to think like your Dad. Whatever happens is meant to be."

Dwayne nodded. "I know what you mean. I think that way a lot."

Dwayne's cell phone rang. He reached for it and pressed voice. "Hello." Dwayne listened, but only heard crying on the other end of the line. He grabbed Melanie's hand and motioned for her to stay for a minute. "Hello. Is someone there? Who is this? Are you all right?"

"Hi Dwayne, it's me, Sharon. Yes, I'm okay, I think, but no, I'm not really okay at all. Oh Dwayne, everything has fallen apart, and I don't know what to do."

"Sharon, don't worry about Mom. The doctor said no damage has been done, and if it's a blood clot, it's treatable."

"I know, Dad told me. It's not Mom." She started to cry again.

"Sharon, what's happened. Are you sick? Is Jeff okay?"

"We're not sick, it's nothing like that. But Dwayne, I think Jeff's seeing another woman."

"No way, what made you think that?"

"He's been calling me from work a couple of times a week, saying he has to work late. I was in town last week and stopped by at 6:30. His boss said he'd left at 5:30 as usual, and hadn't been putting in any overtime as far as he knew. When I got home, Jeff still wasn't there. He finally showed up at 7:30. I didn't say anything. I needed time to think and decide what to do. This week it was the same routine. Yesterday I went out to the car to get a CD from the glove compartment. I noticed a pair of Jeff's jeans, a tee-shirt, and his tennis shoes in the back seat. The shoes had mud on them, and his jeans were torn at the cuffs. The clothes smelled like a stable, but Jeff hates horses and is afraid to get near them, let alone ride one. There was a pair of women's socks with his clothes." Sharon started to cry again. "He must be seeing someone who owns a horse. Dwayne, what should I do? I love Jeff, and I don't want to lose him."

"Wow. I can't believe Jeff is seeing someone else. He loves you too. There must be some other explanation. Why don't you talk to him and ask him what's going on."

"I know I should, but I'm afraid to. I guess I don't want to hear the truth. When I come to visit Mom, can you and I get together alone and talk? Maybe we can make some sense out of this. I don't want to confront Jeff, then find out I've come to the wrong conclusion. I don't want to say anything to Mom and Dad until I know for sure, and have decided what to do. It would just worry them, and they have enough on their minds right now."

"I understand. I'll tell you what, come back to the ranch after you see Mom. With her in the hospital and Dad at the Ellisons, we'll have time to talk. Can Melanie be in on it? She has a good head and may see something that you and I miss."

"Yes, tell Melanie, and Aunt Jody too. I need all the help I can get with this. I'll tell Jeff I'm going to stay over so I can visit Mom."

"That's a good idea. Meanwhile, try not to worry."

"So, are you and Melanie, you know, a thing? Dad said you were fond of her. "

"Melanie is a sweetheart, very smart and very fun to be with. She's Matt Walter's former girlfriend, and yes, I really like her. It's a long story, and I'll tell you all about it when you get here. Bring some jeans. You can go riding with us when we do rounds in the morning."

"Great idea, I sure miss Penny. Is she getting exercised?"

"Lance is seeing to that. He's great with the horses. You'll get to see Anabelle and the kittens too. I'll see you in a day or two, and don't worry."

Dwayne told Melanie about Sharon's concern, and her wanting to talk to them about it. "You know, it's not like Jeff to womanize. He's devoted to Sharon and their marriage. I'm sure something else is going on, although the evidence certainly points to an affair. If he **is** running around on her, I'll have a thing or two to tell him next time I see him."

Melanie frowned. "Poor Sharon, I can imagine how hurt she must feel. I'm glad she's coming. She can tell us all the facts and we can brainstorm what other things might be going on. Maybe we can figure out some more logical reason for those clothes being in Jeff's car."

"I sure hope so. I'll tell Jody after Mom and Dad leave for the hospital. Right now I need to get the folks in cabin four checked out. Do you want to come?"

"No thanks. I'm going to bring my stuff up to the house. I don't relish spending another night with those coyotes." Melanie made a face, and Dwayne kissed her on the forehead.

Chapter 11 - Break In

Melanie put the key in the lock of cabin nine, than realized the door was unlocked. "That's funny," she said out loud. "I'm sure we locked it when we left this morning—hmm, maybe not." She opened the door, but stopped just inside. Something wasn't right. There was a faint scent in the air, something that didn't belong there, something familiar that Melanie couldn't place.

She looked around. Everything was the way they had left it. Or was it? The bed was made, but the quilt was slightly mussed. A corner of it had been lifted up, as if someone had been looking under the bed. That's strange, Melanie thought. Dwayne made the bed before they left, and he was an admitted neatnik. When he made a bed, you could bounce a coin on it. She went into the kitchen and stopped dead. The window over the sink was open, and the screen was torn off. Someone has broken in! Her stomach knotted and she felt a rush of fear wash over her. Wondering if the intruder was still in the cabin, she took off running and didn't stop until she reached the main house. She flew straight into Jody's arms. "There's been a—the window's open—someone looked under the bed."

Jody untangled Melanie's arms. "Wait a minute, slow down. Tell me what happened. Mercy, what on earth scared you so?"

Melanie took a deep breath and struggled to get control. "My cabin's been broken into. Someone tore the screen off and came in the kitchen window." Melanie started toward the door. "I've got to find Dwayne. I don't want him to go down there. Whoever it was may still be in the cabin."

Jody grabbed Melanie's arm. "Wait a minute. Dwayne's down at four checking out the Nelsons. I'll send Marcus to get him. They can take the rifle and go over with Goldie to see what's going on. Melanie, you'd best stay here until they find out what this monkey business is all about."

The screen door opened and Dwayne came in. "What's going on?" he asked, seeing the disturbed looks on their faces.

Melanie ran to him. "Someone's broken into my cabin. The screen's torn off the kitchen window. They were looking for something under the bed. I smelled something strange in the cabin that I couldn't place, something sweet." She stopped for a moment, than remembered. "I know what it was, Polo, the cologne Matt always wears. Oh my gosh, what was he looking for in my cabin, and why didn't he come to the main house?" Melanie was shaking, and close to tears.

Dwayne put his arms around her and held her for a minute. He couldn't imagine Matt breaking in unless he was really out of control. "You know, this is more than we should try to handle ourselves. Matt had to have been pretty strung out to break in. I'm going to call the sheriff."

Dwayne made the call and explained the situation. "We think the person who broke in is Matt Walters, an old friend of mine. Matt's an alcoholic and has done drugs. His ex-girlfriend is staying in the cabin that was broken into."

The deputy instructed Dwayne to stay away from the cabin. "There's a squad car about fifteen minutes from the ranch. They'll meet you at the main house. Lock up and sit tight until they get there. A jealous ex-boyfriend could get pretty nasty if he's been drinking."

Dwayne told the others, and they went to check the doors and windows. The guests were on a field trip, so only the family members were in the house. Melanie curled up on the sofa looking miserable. Jody sat down beside her and took her hand. "Now I know what you must be thinking. First of all, this is not your fault. Matt's got a drinking problem. When he's sober, he's a pleasure to be around. But when he's been drinking, or using those terrible drugs, he can get pretty ugly. We asked him to leave several times when he was out of control."

Melanie nodded. "I know, but I keep thinking I brought all this bad luck on you—Ida's leg, then the coyote, and now this thing with Matt. Maybe none of it would have happened if I hadn't come here."

"Now that's just plain nonsense. Ida's been complaining and hobbling around for weeks. If you hadn't figured out what was going on with her, she might have gotten really sick. As for Matt, he's had problems ever since we've known him. And that coyote certainly wasn't your fault. It was just going after the ducklings. If anything, you've been good luck, and you've certainly been good for Dwayne. I haven't seen him so happy since, well, for a long time. Now you go freshen up, and I'll get Luz to make a fresh pot of coffee. I think we both need a cup." Jody winked. "Maybe we can sneak a little brandy in ours when no one's looking."

Melanie smiled through her tears. "Jody, thank you. I really needed to hear that."

The doorbell rang and Dwayne let in two deputy sheriffs. They introduced themselves as Officers Chavez and Benedetti. They sat down at the kitchen table and pulled out their report pads. "Headquarters filled us in on what was going on up here. Anything else happen since you called in?" Dwayne shook his head. Benedetti pulled out a pencil. "Do any of you have any idea why this Matt Walters would try to break into your place?"

Melanie leaned forward and told her story. "Matt and I were together for a while. Then about a year ago he started drinking heavily. He had temper tantrums over nothing, and said and did inappropriate things. We fought all the time and I finally asked him to leave. He moved out, and I didn't see him for about a year. Then he called last week and arranged to meet me at the farmer's market, but he never showed up. He sent Dwayne after me instead, to tell me he wanted a clean break after all. That's how Dwayne and I met. I didn't know Matt had a history of drug abuse. I also didn't know he'd been married and had two small children." Melanie's eyes welled up with tears.

Dwayne went to her and put his arm around her. "It's okay Mel." He told the officers about how Matt's call ended, and what he'd heard being said in the background.

Benedetti looked at them for a second. "And you two, are you an item now?" There was a long moment of silence. It was the question everyone in the room wanted to hear the answer to. Dwayne spoke up. "We like each other a lot. We've been seeing a lot of each other. Yes, I guess you could call us an item."

"So," Chavez summed up, "Matt sends you to get Melanie. You bring her to the ranch, spend some time together, and fall in love. Then Matt decides he wants her back and follows you here. It's the typical love triangle. But that doesn't explain what he was looking for. What was in the cabin that he might have been interested in?"

"I don't know, unless it was Melanie." They thought for a moment, than Dwayne jumped up. "The gun, maybe he saw us bring the gun to the cabin."

The officers leaned forward, a new look of interest on their faces. "You have a gun? Tell us about it."

Dwayne explained about the coyote, and the pistol he'd brought to the cabin to scare it away. "I was going to shoot over its head, but the coyote never came back. The gun should be right where I left it, in the top dresser drawer."

"Where did you get the gun?" Chavez asked. Dwayne led him to a locked closet where a small locked cabinet housed a rifle and a shotgun. There was an empty place where the pistol had been. "Why do you have the guns? Do you have a permit for them?"

"We have permits for all of them. We rarely use them, but once in a while we need to scare off a coyote, or put down a lame animal. A couple of years back, a stray dog wandered in. He was foaming at the mouth, and went after one our guests. My father shot him. The vet said the dog had rabies. We've had the guns for ages. The gun case and closet are always kept locked."

"Okay. Let's go have a look at that cabin. Dwayne, you come show us where it is. The rest of you stay in the house until we get back. I'm pretty sure your friend took off as soon as he saw us drive up, but lock up just in case."

They got into the sheriff's car and drove to the cabin. The door was still open. Chavez pulled a handkerchief out of his pocket and used it to open the top drawer of the dresser. He looked in the other drawers and turned to the others. "The gun's not here." Dwayne saw the mussed bed and went over to straighten it.

Benedetti caught his arm. "Don't touch anything. This will be a crime scene if you decide to press charges. If that happens, we'll want to dust for prints."

Chavez went into the kitchen, looked at the open window and torn screen, and scribbled some notes on his report. He shut the window, using the handkerchief to preserve any fingerprints, than checked the bathroom. "Let's take a look around outside. Where did you see those marks on the windowpane?" Dwayne led the policemen around the house to the bedroom window. The smudges were still there. "Where did you see the coyote?"

"We never actually saw him, just his markings." Dwayne pointed to the yellow spray marks on the deck. "It left scat in the woods and got a couple of ducklings. The feathers are still scattered around."

Benedetti nodded to Chavez. "Let's take a look in those woods. Dwayne, you stay in the car. Lock her up and lock the cabin." They walked off toward the meadow. Dwayne went around to the front of the cabin, locked the door, and got into the police car. He thought about all that had happened. He couldn't believe Matt had gone to such extremes to find—what? Did he come here looking for Melanie, or me? Did he see us bring the gun to the cabin? Or did he find it when he broke in, and decide it might be useful—but for what? Dwayne put his hands on his forehead. Endless questions without answers whirled around in his head, and an aching behind his eyes threatened to develop into a major headache.

The deputies came back and got into the squad car. "Couldn't find a thing out there, but I'm not surprised. He's probably long gone by now. What does he drive?"

"Matt used to drive a brand new Mercedes. He liked dark colors, green or blue. He traded it every year, but I haven't seen him for a long time. Neither has Melanie, so we don't know what he has now." The deputies asked more questions about where Matt worked and lived, and Dwayne told him what he knew. Chavez handed Dwayne his card. "Here's our phone number. Call us if he shows up or calls. We patrol this area, and can get here pretty quick. I don't want you to take any chances. We take these domestic cases seriously. Too many of 'em end up with someone getting hurt."

Dwayne nodded. "Melanie's things are still in the cabin. Is it all right if I take them? We were going to move her to the main house this morning because of the coyote."

"Good idea." He handed Dwayne the handkerchief. "Try not to touch anything in there." The deputies waited for Dwayne, then drove back to the ranch house and dropped him off. "We're going to hang out near the entrance to the ranch today. You can move around and do whatever needs doing, but be sure to call if anything happens."

Dwayne brought Melanie's things into the house and joined everyone in the kitchen to tell them what the deputies had said. They nibbled the sandwiches Luz had made, but with very little appetite. Dwayne took two aspirins and poured a cup of coffee. "This is a day I could have done without. Let's hope this all gets resolved soon. I'd hate for Mom and Dad to come back to this mess."

They brought Melanie's things into to the East Wing, and Melanie checked her answering machine. There was a message from Izzy. "Hi Mel, how did it go with Matt? Are you back together? Why did he take you to a ranch? I'm having a great time, but I got a little sunburned. There's a bunch of tall men staying at the beach. They belong to a club called the Top Hatters. They're all over six feet, and major hunks, every one of them. I've got my eye on a gorgeous one with the cutest ass. I'll let you know how it goes. Call me, okay? Bye."

Melanie saw the quizzical look on Dwayne's face and explained. "Izzy's my best friend. She's five foot eleven, beautiful and accomplished, but has a hard time meeting men tall enough for her to feel comfortable with. She's published two successful crime/romance novels, and plays a mean game of tennis. Last year she quit her job so she could write full time. I can't wait for you to meet her. I know you'll like her."

Melanie called Izzy back and got her answering machine. "Hi Izzy, its Mel. I've heard of the Top Hatters. Hey, I'm not with Matt. He never showed up. He sent a friend. His name is Dwayne. He's a nice guy, and I really like him." Melanie glanced at Dwayne and winked. "He has a great family. They own this dude ranch. I have lots to tell you. Call me in the morning, I'm usually up early."

Chapter 12 - The East Wing

Dwayne showed Melanie all the nooks and crannies in the east wing. It was a beautiful studio apartment. The sitting room was roomy and comfortable. A used-brick fireplace occupied one wall. There was a wood stove in the bedroom, and the queen-sized canopied bed was covered with another of Ida's quilts. The kitchen had a sink and microwave, and it was fully equipped with dishes, utensils, and some small appliances. The bathroom had a luxurious whirlpool tub. Sliding glass doors in the bedroom opened onto a large deck which had been cut away in one corner to accommodate a huge Poplar tree. Its canopy of leaves shaded the deck. They shimmered and whispered at the slightest breeze, reminding Melanie of the quaking Aspens she'd seen in Colorado. "It's lovely, but I'm so tired, I can't half appreciate it just now. I'm going to lie down for a while."

"I'll join you. I have a splitting headache. Maybe a nap will do us some good." They kicked off their shoes, crawled under the quilt, and dozed off. Melanie woke up first. She propped herself up on one elbow and watched Dwayne sleep, lost in thought about the events of the day. She remembered Dwayne telling the officer they were an item. It was a comfortable thought. She squirmed over and put her arm around Dwayne. He was lying on his side with his back to her. She cuddled closer and kissed his ear. Dwayne stirred, than turned to face her. "Hello. I feel better, how about you?"

"Much better," she said. They held each other close. Dwayne kissed her neck. His lips found hers and Melanie melted into his arms. Their kiss deepened and he stroked her hair.

Dwayne sighed. "You know what. I'm falling in love with you."

"I know, me too. But we hardly know each other. Is it possible? I always thought that love at first sight was only lust."

Dwayne laughed. "Well, I have to admit that I lust you too. But Mel, it's more than that. The more I get to know you, the surer I am that I want you to be in my life. You are beautiful and smart and sweet and fun. I like that you are strong and sensible, yet just a little vulnerable. You're generous, and kind and affectionate, and you bring out the best in me."

"You think I'm affectionate?" Melanie purred. She kissed him again, arousing a passion in both of them that neither wanted to stop. Melanie finally pulled away. She propped her head up with her arm and looked at Dwayne. "And you. You are so much like your father. I was thinking about that last night. You're intelligent and sensitive and caring. You love to have a good time, but in a crisis you're strong and courageous. You have this air of confidence about you, and all the other qualities I've always admired in a man. And sexy—you are the sexiest …"

Dwayne stopped her with a kiss and they held each other for a long time. Dwayne took Melanie's hand. "I can't bear the thought of you leaving when your vacation's over."

Melanie heart skipped a beat. "I've been thinking about that too. With the situation at the hospital, it would be easy to take some time off there, but I still have my business to think of. Gosh, life is so complicated."

Dwayne held her close. They stayed together, talking and laughing and making plans until suddenly Melanie jumped up. "Yoiks, they're gonna set the hounds after us. We're going to have a lot of explaining to do if we go into the main house together."

"Naw, Jody already knows how I feel about you, and she suspects you feel the same. My folks think the sun rises and sets on you, and all the others have been rooting for us from the time they laid eyes on you."

They went back into the main house and found Hilda. "Did Dad call?"

Hilda shook her head. "Not yet. It's been pretty quiet around here compared to this morning. And where did you two disappear to?" Hilda poked Dwayne's arm playfully and winked.

"We took a nap, if you must know." Dwayne laughed and mussed Melanie's hair.

"Well, I don't blame you. We're all plumb worn out from all that sheriff stuff this morning. I sure hope they find Matt and arrest him. I'd be happy if he never shows his face around here again." Hilda bustled back into the kitchen.

The phone rang and Dwayne picked it up. "Hi Dad, how's Mom? What did Doc Elmer say?" He listened for a while. "So Melanie was right. I'll tell everyone. How long will she be in the hospital? Okay. We'll visit her tomorrow afternoon. Do you need anything?"

"I'm okay, but Ida could sure use her robe and slippers, and maybe a nightgown. She keeps complaining about the gown the hospital put her in. She says it's too small and it scratches."

"No problem, we'll bring her some things when we visit."

Dwayne told Melanie and Jody what Tom had said, than went into the kitchen to tell the others. "Mom's had some tests. It's a blood clot all right, called a deep vein thrombosis in medical jargon. It's treatable though. They're going to give her Heparin intravenously for a couple of days. That will thin her blood to help prevent new clots from forming. Then they'll switch her to Warfarin in pill form. The doctor said most clots eventually dissolve on their own, but the medicine will help things go faster. She'll have to stay off her feet for a while, and elevate her legs. And she's going to have to wear some special stockings for a couple of months. Doc said the things you recommended were exactly right, Mel." He put his arm around her and gave her a hug.

The phone rang again. It was Deputy Chavez. "We found Matt. He was doing eighty on the highway traveling south. We'd put an all points out on him because of the stolen gun. He gave the highway patrolman a lot of guff. He claimed he didn't know anything about the gun, and challenged him to search the car. The patrolman didn't find it, and nothing else was out of order. Matt was clean and sober, but ornery as hell. The officer told him a thing or two, and he finally calmed down. He didn't take him in, but he ticketed him for speeding and gave him a warning. It looks like he's headed away from the ranch now, so you can all relax for a while."

"Thanks, we sure appreciate all you've done."

Dwayne told the others and they breathed a sigh of relief. "Poor Matt, that disease has gotten hold of him again. He's a whole other person when he's drinking. Well, since there isn't anything we can do for him, I'm glad he's far away from us. Melanie, I need to go meet the guests who went on the field trip. Do you want to come?"

"No thanks, I want to explore my new digs and decide where to put things." Melanie kissed Dwayne lightly on the lips, and a knowing glance passed between the others.

Dwayne brought the guests back to the ranch. They talked excitedly about the trip they'd taken to the gold country. They'd panned for gold in an old mining town. One of the kids found a gold nugget under a rock in the river. It turned out to be fools gold, but it spurred them on to keep looking. They were determined to find at least one gem, and stayed much later than they planned. Dwayne was happy they'd not been around when the break-in was discovered, and the deputies were there investigating.

After dinner, Dwayne took Melanie for a walk around the grounds to show her the tennis court and swimming pool. "I know. Let's go skinny dipping." Dwayne grinned and started to unbutton his shirt.

Melanie frowned. "I'm not ready for that yet, although it sounds like fun. That hot tub is beckoning to me, but we'd better keep some clothes on. That coyote would really get off at the sight of us."

Dwayne laughed. "Hey—I'm in." He cranked up the heater a couple of notches, and they raced back to the house to get into their bathing suits.

Melanie caught the thermometer that was bobbing around. It registered 102. "Whoa, it's a little toasty." They eased themselves into the water and relaxed, letting the water jets soothe every muscle. "My clients would benefit from this. Some of them have muscles that are so tight, it takes half the session just to get them to relax."

"I'd like to know just what you do to those lucky clients." Dwayne grinned. "Anyway, it's high time I get a sample of this massage therapy stuff."

Melanie beckoned to him. She was sitting on the lower step, covered with water up to her neck. "My pleasure cowboy, come over here and sit with me." Dwayne sidled up to her. She spread her legs and he sat on the step in front of her. She stroked him lightly with both hands all up and down his back. "Now take notes please, 'cause I'm next."

"Don't worry, I'm a quick study." Dwayne wriggled. "Ooh, dat feels good."

"Wait, it gets better." Melanie's touch deepened and she stroked and massaged his shoulders and neck. Dwayne went limp. She worked on his back, than massaged his arms, hands and fingers. Then her touch lightened again, and she ran her hands lightly up and down his back. She placed one hand on his lower back and one on his neck, and held them there for a moment. "Okay, you're done." No answer. Melanie knocked on Dwayne's back. "Hello in there. Is anybody home?" All was quiet. "Hey Dwayne, are you okay?"

Dwayne jumped up and turned to her with a splash. "Aaawoou, its coyote-man, energized by the touch of this lovely lady's talented hands. And boy, am I hungry for woman-flesh!" He pretended to bite her on the neck.

Melanie laughed and splashed him all over. "Okay, coyote-man, now it's my turn. Let's see what you learned." They switched places.

"Now I get to choose where I want to administer therapy on you, right?" Melanie felt Dwayne's hardness pressing close to her. She bopped him on the head. "Now you behave yourself. This is strictly business, no hanky panky, please."

"Oh darn. Okay, here goes." He stroked her shoulders and arms, then his hands moved to her back, and he stroked her softly. His arms stole around her, and she could feel him as he pressed his body close to hers. His hand crept over her thin bathing suit, and he could feel her nipples come to life. Melanie turned to kiss him, a kiss that started softly, than progressed to sweet hungry passion. She was surprised by the depth of her feelings. She'd never felt like this with Matt, or any other man. Her heart beat out of control, and she could feel Dwayne's need for her grow stronger. They held each other and kissed for a long time. Melanie finally drew away and looked down at her hands, saying in a husky voice, "Look, I'm as wrinkled as a prune. You are too."

"The better to eat you, my dear," Dwayne growled, and pretended to bite her again. "But you're right, I guess its time to get out." He climbed out of the tub, dried off, and wrapped a bath towel around his waist, then grabbed a towel for Melanie. She got out and he dried her off, than quickly wrapped the towel all the way around her, trapping her arms in the cocoon.

Melanie's eyes twinkled. "You are a dickens." Dwayne laughed and kissed her lightly, than twirled her out as the towel unrolled. Melanie went after Dwayne and tried to catch him with the towel. He ran backwards, and teetered on the edge of the hot tub. Melanie caught him just as he was about to fall in. They wrestled and laughed, and ended up locked together in each others arms. They held each other for a long time, then put on terrycloth robes and sandals, and walked back to the east wing. Millions of stars twinkled above them, and the moon was whole, except for a small sliver that was covered in shadow.

Chapter 13 – Town

Dwayne and Melanie got up early the next morning. They saddled Danny and Jenny and did their morning scout of the ranch, ending at cabin nine. There was no further evidence of coyote activity, but when they looked inside the cabin, Melanie felt cold prickles down her back. They stayed only a minute, than rode back to the stables. Dwayne gave the horses a handful of oats and turned them over to Lance.

Dwayne brushed some hay off Melanie and kissed the tip of her nose. "Mom's having tests so she's not available for visitors until this afternoon, but I'd like to drive into town early and do some shopping. Mom needs a new robe and slippers and Mel, you should get some ranch duds."

"Me? No, I have everything I need for now."

"Nonsense, you can't keep running around in those tennis shoes—you'll wear them out. Besides, if you step in a cowflop, you'll be out of luck."

Melanie laughed. "No prob. If that happens, I'll just give them to you to clean."

Dwayne put his hands up. "No way, there's a boot shop near the hospital, and you need a hat too. When we're done shopping, there are some fun places to eat lunch."

Melanie shook her head. "Lunch sounds great Dwayne, but I just bought a new suit and a pair of shoes at Nordstroms. My clothing budget is zilch until I pay them off. It'll be fun to look at everything though."

"I'd really like to buy you a pair of boots and a cowboy hat. It would give me much pleasure."

Melanie crossed her arms over her chest. "I can't let you buy all those things for me. You're sweet to want to, but it just doesn't feel right."

Dwayne took Melanie's hands and backed her up against one of the stalls. "Mel, you and I are a couple now. I meant what I said about loving you, and wanting us to be together forever. I want to share everything with you, my love and my home, and whatever else I own. I hope you feel that way too."

"I do, Dwayne. It's just that it's all so new. It will take some getting used to. I am certain of one thing though. I love you too, and want to spend the rest of my life with you."

Dwayne took Melanie's hand and kissed her fingers, then turned her hand over and kissed her palm. "Then we're committed. So, now can I buy you a proper hat and boots?"

Melanie smiled. "Okay cowboy. But I already feel like, how did Ida put it? I'm already feeling right spoiled." Dwayne laughed, and they walked arm in arm back to the house.

Melanie saw the light blinking on her answering machine and pressed the button. "Hey, Mel, it's Izzy. Tag, you're it. Darn, I really wanted to talk to you. I slept in this morning. We went out last night. Bruce is really cool, and very romantic. He's an attorney, and a real gentleman. But I want to hear about you. Call me when you can. Bye."

Melanie called Izzy back and got her answering machine again. "Hi Izzy, this is the longest game of phone tag I've ever played. I want to hear all about your guy, and have lots to tell you too. We'll catch up when we connect. Meanwhile, have fun and be careful."

The first stop in town was Country Fashions, a clothing store with a little of everything. They chose a robe and slippers for Ida in soft blue fleece, with a matching flowered nightgown. Dwayne paid for them while Melanie sauntered through the store. She looked at the western-style jeans, and belts with big decorative buckles. Most of the shirts were western cut, with metal brads sewn on in patterns—nothing like anything she owned. She stopped at a rack of low-cut blouses in soft pastels with long, full, crinkled skirts to match. She pulled the green one off the rack to look at the price tag.

Dwayne joined her. "You should try that one on. You'd look great in it. It almost matches your eyes."

Melanie took the dress to the fitting room. She emerged twirling and dancing, and stopped in front of Dwayne. "Howdy partner, how do I look?"

Dwayne bowed deeply. "Melanie, you look superb. The color is perfect on you. Please let me get it for you." His face wore that pleading look that Melanie found so hard to resist.

"All right cowboy. When you look at me like that, I'm a pushover." Dwayne kissed her, and she went back to the dressing room to change.

The next stop was the Livery. Melanie tried on several cowboy hats. She chose a perky beige one with a small wooden horseshoe that slid up under her chin to hold the hat in place. The boots were harder to choose. Melanie had never owned cowboy boots, and the pointy toes pinched. She finally found a pair that fit, and had to admit they looked pretty sharp. She looked in the mirror. "Hey, look at me. I'm off to the rodeo." She hugged Dwayne and thanked him, but the look in his eyes told her she was all the thanks he needed.

"Say, are you hungry? There's an old-fashioned drug store on the corner with a soda fountain. We can get a sandwich and a chocolate soda and bring Mom some penny candy. This drug store's the only place in town that still sells something for a penny."

"Sounds like a plan. I love chocolate sodas, and haven't had one for ages."

The drug store was picturesque. The boy behind the counter wore a white shirt and red bow tie. The floor was done in big black and white checkerboard tiles, and the high, red-leather stools twirled all the way around. The food was good. They each came away with a handful of spice drops, and a package of saltwater taffy for Ida.

At the hospital, Dwayne asked the receptionist for Ida's room number and they went upstairs. Tom was there, and came over to hug them. "Hi Dad. Mom, how are you feeling?" Dwayne kissed his mother, and Melanie gave her the taffy.

"My leg's much better, but you've got to get me out of this place. They've stabbed and poked and fussed over me 'til I'm fit to be tied. They hooked me up to this tube, and kept waking me up all night to ask if I was okay. Yesterday a nurse tried to give me an enema! I told her to get out of my room with that nasty contraption. Then she looked at the chart and said 'oops, sorry dear.' Turned out the enema was for the girl next door." Dwayne and Melanie giggled, and Tom turned away so Ida couldn't see him laughing. "And look at this gown they've put me in. It's not big enough to cover a Barbie doll." Ida blushed and drew the covers up over the skimpy hospital gown.

"We brought you a remedy for that." Dwayne handed her the shopping bag and Ida held the gown and robe to her chest. "Now that's more like it. These are pretty and so soft—and they're decent, thank you son. Tom, help me get into these things." Tom tried to control his laughter as he unbuttoned the robe.

Dwayne and Melanie went to look for the doctor. They found a nurse and asked if Dr. Elmer was around. "You just missed him, but I can have him paged. I'm sure he'll want to talk to you."

While they waited, a pregnant woman walked by. "Let's go see the babies," Melanie whispered.

They followed the woman to the maternity ward. The newborns were adorable. They were awake, and kept the two nurses busy feeding and changing them. One of the nurses held up twins to show their parents, who were watching through the window. She pointed to Dwayne and Melanie, then to the other babies. "Is one of them yours?" she mouthed.

Melanie shook her head. "No, we're just looking." Dwayne took Melanie's hand, and they were both lost in thought as they walked back to Ida's room.

The doctor was there, and he greeted Dwayne and Melanie warmly. Ida had told him all about Dwayne's charming new friend, and the doctor was happy that he was finally seeing someone again. He shuffled through the papers on Ida's chart. "I just got the last of the test results and they confirmed what we already suspected. The blood clot is small, and it's treatable. The drugs will help prevent others from forming. But the tests also show that Ida's blood pressure is significantly elevated. I want her to stay here at least a couple of days to regulate that, and to continue the Heparin I.V. Then we can send her home with some tablets if she promises to follow my instructions. You'll have to keep a sharp eye on her. She has a mind of her own."

"You can say that again," laughed Tom. "Don't worry. If she gets out of line, I'll give her a good strapping, then Luz'll make her drink down some of that green tea she sets such a store on. Ida hates that tea worse than an enema."

Ida sat up straight in bed and made a face at Tom. "Now don't you all be talking about me as if I wasn't right here in this room. Doc, did you know that yesterday a nurse tried to give me an enema that belonged to the girl next door?"

The doctor threw up his hands in exasperation. "Sorry about that mix-up. Sometimes the nurses get overworked. I'll talk to her and tell her to be more careful. I've got to go now. I have several other patients to see this afternoon."

Chapter 14 - Sharon

Dwayne shook Dr. Elmer's hand and thanked him, and the doctor turned and almost collided with Sharon. He caught her in a hug. "Hello. What a treat, it's so nice to see you. You're looking great."

Sharon drew back and smiled. "It's good to see you too. It's been ages. How's Mom?" She looked past the doctor and saw Dwayne and Tom standing around Ida. She hated seeing her mother in a hospital bed. She was used to seeing her running around fixing this and taking care of that. She went to her mother and hugged her, than gathered the others into a group hug. A tear slipped out, but she quickly wiped it away, than hugged Ida again. "Hi Mom, how are you feeling? Is your leg any better?" She touched Ida's bathrobe. "Say, is this new? What a pretty color," and she rubbed the soft fabric of the bathrobe between her fingers.

"I'm okay, but I've got a blood clot. That's what's been causing all the pain. This tube is dripping something in me to help dissolve it. Ida grabbed Sharon in another hug. It's so good to see you honey. We sure do miss you."

Dr. Elmer picked up Ida's chart. "I really have to go. Ida's doing fine. If you all will fill Sharon in on the details, I'd appreciate it. I'll check back with you later."

Ida introduced Melanie to Sharon and told her story, starting with Melanie finding the blood clot during her examination. "She's a smart one, she is. Thanks be to God that she was visiting right now, or I might've been in much worse shape. I'm mighty grateful." Ida reached for Melanie's hand and drew her over to the bed. "Dwayne, you'd better hang on to this girl, or someone else is going to grab her away from you."

Dwayne smiled. "I know, Mom, and don't you worry, I won't let that happen. We should take off now, and check on things at the ranch. Dad, are you okay over at the Ellisons?"

Tom scowled. "Yeah, Ted's beaten me at checkers ten times, but I think I'm on to him now. Tonight's gonna be my game. You two take care and drive carefully. I'll see you in a couple of days."

Dwayne hugged his sister. "Bye Sharon, we'll talk more at the ranch. Try to get back by dinner. Gee, it's sure good to see you."

It wasn't until Dwayne and Melanie climbed into the pickup that they remembered they hadn't mentioned any of the ruckus about Matt breaking in and stealing the gun. "You know, it's probably just as well. There's no point in telling them more bad news when they already have so much on their minds. We'll fill them in when they get home. I hope by then it will all be resolved."

Dwayne gathered everyone together when they got back and told them the news about Ida. "Sharon's in town. She was at the hospital. She'll be here for dinner."

Luz went into the kitchen and pulled out her recipe for carrot cake. It was Sharon's favorite. She checked the refrigerator and saw she had enough cream cheese for the frosting. There was just enough time to bake the cake before the leg of lamb went into the oven.

Melanie started thinking about the layoffs at the hospital. She wondered if she'd been notified by mail. She found her cell phone and called her landlady. "Hi Rhonda, its Melanie. I'm on vacation at a dude ranch up north. Would you do me a favor? Look in my mailbox and tell me if there's a letter from the hospital."

"Sure, just a minute." Rhonda left the phone and returned a minute later. "There's a letter from the administrative office. Do you want me to read it to you?"

"Yes, please." Melanie held her breath as Rhonda read: "Dear Ms. Parks. Funding for the hospital has been cut again, and we have been unable to meet our budget for the past several years. There is a possibility that some of our nursing staff may have to be laid off. You are invited to come to a general meeting to discuss these issues on July 22nd at 4:00pm in the hospital auditorium. I hope to see you there."

"Wow!" Rhonda sounded concerned. "That doesn't sound good at all. Do you think you're going to be laid off?"

"I don't know. I'm going to arrange to get back for the meeting. I'll tell you more when I see you Friday. Is there any news from your daughter?"

"She's had some twinges, but no real labor yet. Laurie's enormous, but it's all baby. She's carrying it all in front, and the baby's dropped. When you see her from the back, or the waist up, you hardly know she's pregnant. She told me the funniest story. She stopped for lunch in a crowded deli. A man came over and asked if he could share her table. She said sure, and he sat down across from her. After they'd talked for a while, he asked if she would like to go out with him. She stood up and showed him her nine-month belly, and the man almost fell off his chair. He stammered and stuttered an apology, and Laurie went off laughing."

"So he hit on her, and he didn't even know she was pregnant. That's so funny. I'll bet she'll be glad when that baby comes. Thanks for the info about the hospital, Rhonda. I'll let you know what's happening."

Melanie sat down to think. She felt like she was on a fast-moving jet. Everything was happening too fast, and there were too many things to decide. But she knew this bit with the hospital wasn't necessarily bad news. She needed a break from her hectic nursing job. If she didn't get laid off, maybe she should just give notice. And with things progressing so fast with her and Dwayne, maybe she should tell Sara and Paula they might have to start interviewing for a new partner. She knew they would miss her, and she would miss them too, but they'd be happy to hear about her and Dwayne. Melanie smiled at the thought, than scowled when she realized that would leave her without income. Maybe I can get a job at the hospital in Sonora. Or open a massage studio up here. She put her head in her hands. It made her dizzy to think of all that had happened in such a short period of time. She wished she could connect with Izzy. Her friend always seemed to be able to see the big picture, and had a way of helping her sort things out, and put them in perspective. Dwayne found her pacing up and down, trying to figure things out. Melanie told him about the hospital. "I need to go back for the meeting. Can you drive down with me?"

"I'd love to, but I can't leave the ranch with Mom and Dad both away. It's near the end of the season, and some of the families will be leaving. Anabelle's twins are due any time, and the vet said it's likely to be a difficult delivery. And with Sharon here, and all this unsettled mess with Matt, I need to stick around and see to things. Do you mind driving back alone? We have an extra car you could take, an Oldsmobile that's comfortable and runs well."

Melanie frowned. "Darn, I was hoping you could come with me." Just a minute, let me think." She was quiet for a moment. "You know, it might be better for me to take a bus, or the Amtrak. Then I can drive my car back. I'll check the schedules."

Sharon arrived at the ranch just before dinner. The family surrounded her, hungry for news about her job, her new swimming pool, and the pie contest she'd just won. Sharon filled them in, and only Dwayne and Melanie noticed she omitted saying anything about Jeff. "Gee, it is so good to be home again. I sure miss this place."

Luz offered Sharon another slice of cake. "We miss you too. The ranch just isn't the same without you. Was that my recipe you used to make that pie? I'd sure be pleased if it was."

"Yes, it was your chocolate cream pie. I added half a package of melted dark chocolate chips and sprinkled some shaved chocolate on top of the whipped cream. I called it double delight chocolate cream pie. It was so rich, you could only eat a small piece at a time. Jeff loved it. He's a chocoholic. The pie that took second prize was yummy too. Amy won it with her apple/walnut/ginger pie with the crisscross crust."

After dinner, Melanie, Dwayne, and Sharon went up to the barn to see the horses. Sharon smiled when she saw Penny, and threw her arms around her. Penny was a beautiful chestnut with a white nose. When she saw Sharon, she whinnied and nuzzled her. "Hey girl, how are you doing? Do you miss me? Remember all the good times we had, riding with the wind." Sharon turned to Melanie. "Jeff is afraid of horses, so I don't get a chance to go riding unless I do it alone, or come to the ranch. He's had nightmares about falling off a horse, although he doesn't remember riding as a kid. He thinks he must have blocked out some incident in his childhood."

They went over to see the kittens. Sharon sat down on the hay. She picked up Tiger and put her on her lap. "Well aren't you the proud mama. I guess we all know what you've been doing." She petted the cat's soft head and scratched behind her ears. Tiger settled down and purred loudly in response.

Dwayne and Melanie sat down next to Sharon. The kittens came over to play, batting the strands of hay, and anything else that moved. Sharon sneezed, and the orange kitten jumped high in the air, arching her back. She landed on all four paws, than walked daintily away with her tail in the air as if nothing had happened. Dwayne laughed. "What a clown. She's our favorite. So Sharon, what's going on? Have you found out anything new since we talked?"

Sharon sighed. "It's the same routine. Every Tuesday and Thursday Jeff calls and says he's working overtime. He gets home around 7:30, says he's starving, and wolfs down his dinner. I've noticed a faint horse odor on him too. Whoever she is, she's definitely around horses a lot. Other than that, things seem normal between us. Jeff is attentive and affectionate. He took me out to celebrate winning the pie contest, and we had a wonderful time. We're going on a cruise to Alaska in the fall, and he's still excited about that. My birthday's coming up, and he told me he has a surprise for me. If it's a party, I don't know how I can handle that. I'm at my wits end. I've even considered hiring a private detective to follow him. Then I'd know for sure one way or the other. I can't stand being up in the air, and I don't know how to act with him any more. I can't keep hiding how hurt and angry I am, but I'm afraid to ask him. Do either of you have any advice?"

Dwayne nodded. "I still think the best thing to do is confront him. Just ask him outright. You'll be able to see by his body language if he's telling the truth."'

Melanie thought for a minute, than jumped up. "This is a long shot, but here goes. You said Jeff is afraid of horses, but he knows how much you love them, and love to ride. What if he's going to a therapist to cure him of his fear, or maybe he's taking riding lessons to please you."

Sharon's face brightened. "Wow. I never thought of that. That would explain why he hasn't changed how he acts with me. And if he's been riding after work, that's why he smells of horses, and is so hungry when he gets home. Say, maybe that's what his birthday surprise is. You know, just hoping there's an explanation for everything, other than a love affair, makes me feel so much better. Gosh, I need to figure out what to do next. Should I wait for my birthday? It's just a week away, but I'll be on pins and needles. On the other hand, if I confront him now, and your guess is right, I'll blow his surprise. I think I'll wait."

Dwayne caught Sharon in a hug, and Sharon drew Melanie into the circle. "Thank you, Melanie. I feel so much better. What did Aunt Jody say?"

"I didn't tell her yet. There's so much going on, I didn't get a chance."

"It's just as well. Jody would worry too much. And now that there's a possible explanation, I may never have to say a word to her, or to Mom and Dad. That would suit me fine. You know what, I'm going to drive back tonight instead of staying over. I see that Mom's being well taken care of, and isn't in any danger. I want to get back to Jeff and see how it feels to be with him now that I don't have that anger inside. I'm afraid I've been pretty distant for the last couple of weeks, and have probably hurt his feelings. If your theory is right, he's probably wondering what's eating me."

Dwayne smiled. "That's a good idea. Who knows, if Melanie is right, on your next visit with Jeff, you might be able to go riding together."

Sharon sighed. "That would be so great." She stopped to say goodbye to Penny, and gave her another hug, then they walked back to the house. Sharon said goodbye to the family, and Luz gave her the rest of the carrot cake to take back to Jeff.

Chapter 15 – Tie Breaker

Melanie went back to the east wing and sat down in the rocking chair. Her mind was going a hundred miles a minute. Dwayne found her there. He went around behind her and massaged her shoulders. "A penny for your thoughts."

Melanie laughed. "No way, these are major issues I'm mulling over. You'll have to offer a lot more than that."

Dwayne frowned. "I guessed that by the serious look on your face. Say, if you haven't been laid off, would you consider resigning so you can come and live here with me?"

Melanie smiled. "I've had some thoughts about that too, but right now I'm so tired, I can't think straight. So much has happened, I feel like I'm in a silent movie."

Dwayne laughed. "I know what you mean. Come to bed. What you need is a good night's sleep. We both do." He took her hands, pulled her up out of the chair and held her close. "I love you Melanie. I'm sorry all this is happening, but it will soon be behind us, and we can begin our life together. Can I stay with you tonight?"

Melanie smiled sleepily. "That would be nice. I know we'll be good. We're too tired not to be."

Melanie was asleep before Dwayne finished his shower. He crawled quietly under the covers, being careful not to disturb her, and they slept soundly until dawn. Dwayne stirred first, and crept out of bed to use the bathroom. Melanie was right behind him. They both shivered in the morning air and jumped back under the covers. Dwayne drew Melanie into his arms. He kissed her ear and whispered "Hello my sweet," then gently kissed her lips. She put her arms around him and kissed him back, and they fell back asleep entwined in each others arms.

After breakfast, Melanie called Amtrak and reserved a seat on a train that was leaving Friday morning. She sighed as she told Dwayne about her plans. "It'll be close, but I can just make the meeting at the hospital at four. I hope it won't last too long. I'll take a cab from the train to the hospital."

Dwayne thought for a moment. "I'll drive you to the station. Gosh, I wish I could go with you. Just when you need my support, I'm stuck here at the ranch."

"It's okay. I have a lot of running around to do, and the quiet time on the train will be useful. I need to think and make plans. It's been such a whirlwind, and I have a lot of decisions to make. I want to spend some time with Sara and Paula too, and tell them about us."

Dwayne nodded. "It's going to be a long three days. Nothing will be the same without you."

"I know. I'm going to miss you too."

They saddled Jenny and Danny and did their morning rounds. They left the horses with Lance, than checked on Anabelle. She was chewing on some grass. She looked up at them with her big brown eyes as if to say hey, let's get on with it. Get these babies out of me. Dwayne and Melanie caught the look. They scratched her silky ears and promised that delivery day would be soon. Their next stop was the barn to see Tiger and the kittens. They were full of energy. They climbed all over each other and batted each other's tails. Melanie picked up the orange one. "Are they really all promised?"

Dwayne laughed as one of the kittens tried to climb up his boot. "Families put in their reservations as soon as we announced Tiger was expecting. Tiger's a special cat. We've never figured out who her mate is, but they always produce first class kittens. We're going to keep one of them as a house pet. Tiger's an outdoor cat. She's happiest roaming the ranch and catching mice."

Melanie picked up each kitten and stroked its soft fur. "How can we choose just one? They're all so cute."

"Their personalities will develop in a couple of weeks. Then it'll be easier." Dwayne picked up the orange kitten. "So far I'm partial to this little guy, but we'll see. We have some time before lunch. Are you up to a friendly game of tennis?"

Melanie's eye's sparkled. "You bet." They went back to the house and changed into tennis clothes. Dwayne donned a Nike shirt and shorts. Melanie wore a saucy blue tennis skirt and a white scoop-neck shirt. A pair of fluffy blue balls that were attached to her socks dangled over the heels of her tennis shoes. She opened a can of yellow balls and dropped them into the pockets that were hidden in her skirt.

Dwayne whistled when he saw her. "No fair. How am I going to concentrate on the game with you looking like that?"

"Not to worry, you'll probably beat the pants off me. I haven't played for a while." They brought their rackets and some bottled water over to the court. They rallied back and forth for a while, and Melanie found herself running after a lot of balls. "Whew! I'm really out of practice. And you, you're really good! Want to play a game?"

"Sure." Dwayne dropped a ball and sent it over the net. Melanie won the rally, and whacked the first serve out of the court. She served again. The ball spun high in the air and landed in the inside corner of the service area. Dwayne ran after it, but it curved out of his reach. He scooted up closer to the net. Melanie's next serve pounced up in the air, than landed on the line just inside the service area. Dwayne connected, but hit too hard. The ball went flying past Melanie and out of the court. Melanie served again. This time the ball barely cleared the net. It landed near the line, than curved out of the court before Dwayne could get to it. "Good serve," he called.

Melanie managed to stay neck and neck with Dwayne until the end. Dwayne had the power advantage, but Melanie was able to place the ball exactly where she wanted it, so she was able to hold her own on the rallies. Dwayne had a good serve, but when Melanie managed to return it, she waited for her chance, then rushed to the net and smashed a lob into a far corner. Her powder puff serve threw him off, and he either misjudged where it landed, or over-hit. Dwayne finally won the tie breaker. "You play a great game, Mel. What a wicked serve. It curves all over the place, and I never know where it's going to land."

Melanie bowed. "Thanks. I had to develop something strategic to offset my lack of power. That was fun, but now I'm hungry. Let's go see what Luz has conjured up."

Dwayne picked up the balls. "That sounds good. I'm famished."

During dinner, Dwayne could see that Melanie was preoccupied. She was unusually quiet, and Tom had to ask her twice to pass the butter. After dinner, she excused herself and disappeared into the east wing. Dwayne found her sitting in the chair again, staring into space. "What's wrong, Mel? Did I say something to hurt your feelings?"

Melanie stood up. "No, no, it's nothing like that. It's just that my mind is a jumble of half-made plans. There have been so many changes in my life in such a short period of time. It seems impossible to make sense out of anything. And now I'm going home, possibly to face a major career change that will leave me without income. It's all so overwhelming."

Dwayne drew Melanie over to the bed, and sat down next to her. "I understand how you feel. Both of our lives have changed since we met, but my changes are easy to deal with. I can stay right here and invite you into my life without batting an eye. But I'm asking you to give up your work, your friends, and your apartment, and take a chance on living here with me. But Melanie, please know that, although we've only known each other a short time, I love you very much, and I want us to spend the rest of our lives together. I know that we'll make each other happy. Wait—I want to do this right." Dwayne kneeled down in front of Melanie and took her hand. "Melanie, will you marry me, and come to live with me here at the ranch? Please say yes." The old pleading look on Dwayne's face caused Melanie to smile, in spite of the seriousness of the moment. Dwayne saw the look, and was afraid he'd spoken too soon. "Oh oh, I hope you don't think it's…"

Melanie put her fingers to his lips. "Yes. The answer is definitely yes, I want to marry you. I can't bear the thought of our not being together. I love you too. It's the only thing I'm sure of right now. I just need to untangle the rest of my life so I can come back here to start a new one with you."

Dwayne put his arms around Melanie and let out a deep sigh. "You've made me very happy. I didn't want to rush you, but I wanted to make it official before you leave. I didn't want you changing your mind as soon as I was out of sight!"

Melanie laughed. "Not a chance. And the untangling will seem a little easier, now that I know where it's all going. You know, we are so lucky. Just think what would have happened if Matt had shown up at the farmers' market? I might never have met you, or found out about him."

"Yes. I'm sure he has no idea what a big favor he did for us when he asked me to pick you up. Say, let's not tell the others about us until you get back and the folks are home. I'd like to tell everyone together. I would like to tell Sharon though, if it's okay with you. She'll be happy for us, and she'll keep it quiet until we're ready to tell the others."

Melanie nodded. "Hey Dwayne, remember when I grabbed you and hugged you when you first showed me the deck behind cabin nine? I'll never forget the look on your face. I thought I'd made a big mistake, and that you were thinking I was a brazen hussy. I had already started to like you a lot, and for a minute, I thought I'd lost my chances. Then later, when you walked me back to the cabin and hugged me, I was so relieved."

"That hug sure did feel good, and I also remember how good it felt when you fell asleep on my shoulder in the truck on the way to the ranch. The smell of your hair and the warmth of your body drove me crazy. I love you so much." They kissed and held each other until they finally fell asleep in each other's arms.

The next day was a busy one. Melanie made a list of the people she needed to contact, and all the things she had to do. There were so many areas of her life that would change. It was exciting, but also scary. She would miss her friends, and the people she worked with. But she was ready to give up the hectic lifestyle she'd fallen into. With her full-time nursing job, and the massage studio, there hadn't been much time to just enjoy life. She loved being with Dwayne, and treasured the fun times they'd had. It was exciting to know that their life at the ranch would continue, and that his family would become hers. She smiled at that thought. She hadn't had family around her for a long time, and Dwayne's family were such good people. She finally decided to stop planning, and just let things happen.

Part III

Chapter 16 – The Journey

Melanie stirred in her sleep. She turned over onto her left side and stretched one arm over her head. She felt Dwayne cuddle up close to her. He kissed her ear, and ran his hand softly up and down her shoulder. She could feel his warm breath on her neck. She sighed and snuggled closer. His arm circled around her and he fondled her. Then suddenly, his hand crept up to her throat and tightened around it. He was holding her hard—squeezing her. She struggled and grabbed his hand, but couldn't free herself. "Hey!" She cried out. "I can't breathe. Stop it, let go!" She finally wriggled out of his grip and turned to face him. She opened her eyes and saw—Matt! It was Matt, not Dwayne who was next to her, touching her, choking her. "No. Stop. You're hurting me. Go away." She tried to move, but he grabbed her arm.

"Hey lady—**lady**, wake up. You having a bad dream." Melanie awoke with a start. A young girl was leaning toward her, shaking her arm. "Wake up Ma'am. Look here, no one's hurtin' you. You was calling out like someone was killin' you. But look, no one's in these seats but you and me. That must have been a bad nightmare."

Melanie was fully awake now. She sat up straight and put her hand to her throat, than looked at the girl next to her. "I was having a terrible dream. I'm sorry if I scared you." She looked around to see if anyone else had heard, but the other passengers all had their faces buried in books, or were dozing in their seats. "Thank you for waking me. It was so real. I could feel him choking me."

"Who was doin' that to you. Say, I bet you're running away just like me. Man, I'm so glad to get away from there. My Momma, she just wouldn't believe he came after me. She thought I made it all up. It's a good thing Aunt Nettie said I could come stay with her. Otherwise I'd of had no place to go. Are you okay now Ma'am?"

Melanie sat up in her seat and looked at the girl. "I'm fine. It was just a dream. Who are you running away from? Does your mother know where you're going? By the way, my name's Melanie, what's yours?"

"I'm Moesha. Yeah. Momma knows. She sent me to live with Aunt Nettie, and got me this train ticket. I think she knew he was after me, but she didn't want to look at it. She lets him hang around because he pays the rent and buys her stuff. I told her I could quit school and get a job so she could kick him out, but she wouldn't listen."

"I'm glad you didn't quit school. How old are you?"

"I'm fifteen. If I stay in school, I'll graduate next year. I have pretty good grades, except for English, but every time I sit down to study, that old Duke comes nosing around. He keeps putting his hands on me, touching my hair, and talkin' that sweet talk. You could get high just smelling his breath. Some days he drinks all day long." Moesha held her nose and made a face. "Last week when Momma was at work, he followed me into my bedroom. He took my new dress out of the closet and told me to put it on. I'll tell you, I was so scared. I knew what he was up to. I'd heard him carrying on about that dress to Momma, saying it cost too much and was too grown up for me. I said no, but he came right up to me and started unbuttoning my blouse. Man, I freaked! I would have hit him, but just then Momma came home and he skedaddled out of my room. I tried to tell her about it later. At first she didn't believe me. But the next day she asked me about it again. Then she asked me if I wanted to go live with Aunt Nettie for a while. I said yes right away. Aunt Nettie lives near the hospital. She's got a good job there. They're laying off a lot of people, but she's been there a long time so she'll probably get to stay on."

"Wow, Moesha, what a terrible thing you have been through. I'm so glad your mother is sending you to a safe place. I work at the hospital too, or used to."

"Are you one of those people that got laid off?"

"I'm not sure yet." Melanie looked at her watch. "I'm on my way to the hospital now to find out. I've been on vacation. I got a letter telling about the layoffs, so I came back to go to the meeting. It starts at four. I'll just make it if the train's on time, and if I can catch a cab to the hospital."

"Hey, my aunt will give you a ride. It'll be quicker than trying to get a cab." Moesha looked out the window. "Look, we're almost there."

"That's really kind of you. Are you sure your Aunt won't mind? What's her last name? Maybe I know her."

"Her name's Nettie Williams. She won't mind. She's a good person. My uncle died a couple of years ago. She was feeling mighty low for a while, but she kept on working and supporting herself. I wish Mom would get a better job and get rid of that no good Duke. Then I could go home again." Moesha pulled out a wrinkled tissue and wiped at her tears.

Melanie patted her hand. "It's really hard when things go wrong at home. My parents died when I was just a couple of years older than you. I wanted to go to nursing school. I got a student loan and part-time job and finally got my degree. I was on my own for a long time, but I just met a wonderful man."

"Is he the one that's been beatin' on you? If he is, you better get away from him quick. It seems like when a man's no good, he never does get any better, and sooner or later you're gonna get hurt really bad!"

"No, it's not Dwayne. He's the sweetest, gentlest man I've ever known. He wouldn't hurt a flea. My nightmare was about an old boyfriend who also drinks too much. He gets mean when he drinks, and I think he's angry about my going with this other fellow. Matt never really hurt me in real life, just in my dreams."

The train blew a long whistle and started to decelerate, then pulled into the station. Moesha saw her aunt standing on the platform. "Look, there she is. There's Aunt Nettie." They stood up and made their way through the train.

Nettie waived. "Moesha, I'm over here." Melanie went down the stairs and watched as Moesha's aunt gathered her up in a big hug. "Well, look at you. You are all grown up, and as pretty as can be. I am so happy to see you. I've worried myself sick about you living there under those circumstances. Thank goodness your mother finally let you come to live with me." Nettie hugged Moesha again, than noticed Melanie standing nearby. "Hello" she said.

"Hello. My name is Melanie Parks. I sat next to your niece on the train, and we got to talking. She told me you worked at the hospital. I work there too, and was on my way to the meeting. Moesha said you might give me a ride. If you would be so kind, I would really appreciate it. I don't think I'll make it on time if I wait for a cab."

Nettie reached out and shook Melanie's outstretched hand. "So you work at the hospital too. I'm so pleased to meet you, and of course I'd be happy to give you a ride. I saw this coming for a long time, with all the cuts they've done in the last couple of years, and I'm anxious to know if my job was affected. I don't think I'm going to get laid off because I have a lot of seniority, but I want to hear what they have to say, and whether my hours will be changed."

They drove to the hospital and found a parking space on the edge of the lot. "Moesha, there's a cafeteria down the hall. Why don't you wait for me there. They have some magazines, and you can get a snack from the vending machines. After the meeting we'll go back to my place and get you settled. I have beef stew simmering in the crock pot, and dumplings all made and ready to pop on top."

The meeting hall was packed, and the administrator spoke about the budget cuts the hospital had been facing. He outlined some cost-cutting plans they were going to put in place. "Unfortunately that won't be enough. We're going to have to lay off some of our staff. We'll honor those that have seniority, so the last people hired will be the first to go. A list is posted on the bulletin board. You'll be eligible for COBRA health insurance, and you'll be hired back before we take on outside people. Those of you who are staying may have to put in some extra hours, but we'll try to rotate so no one will have to put in too much overtime."

Melanie and Nettie followed the group of downcast employees and found the list of layoffs. Neither of their names were on it. Nettie took a deep breath. "Well that's good. How about you? Are you able to put in some extra time?"

"Actually, I'm on my way to human resources to submit my resignation. I'm going to move up north and live on a ranch with my boyfriend. That's where I was coming from when I met Moesha."

"That sounds very exciting. I'm so glad I finally got to meet you, after all these years of working at the same hospital. I have to find Moesha now, and get her home and settled. It was really nice talking to you, and I wish you the very best."

Melanie shook Nettie's hand. "I'd like to keep in touch with you. Here's my phone number." Melanie wrote her number on her business card. "Good luck to you. And tell Moesha to stay in school."

"I will, goodbye." Nettie waved and disappeared down the hall.

Melanie handed her letter of resignation to the human resources director. "What's this? You're resigning? You weren't on the layoff list, were you?"

"No. I came prepared to resign, no matter what I heard at the meeting. I met this wonderful man. He owns a dude ranch up north, and I'm going up there to be with him."

"Well aren't you the lucky one. What happened to that other guy, what's his name—Matt something? Weren't you two an item for a while?"

"That ended a year ago, and it's a good thing as it turned out. But that's a long story I'll tell you some other time. I need to turn in my keys and badge, and pick up my COBRA papers. I'll be leaving in a couple of days."

"Let us know if you ever need a reference." She handed Melanie some papers. "Good luck, and come to see us some time."

Melanie left the office, than remembered the stinky cell phone that was still in her apartment. She came back and tried to explain what happened to it. The story sounded ludicrous, like a scene from a movie, and they both ended up laughing. "I'll bring it back in a day or two. Maybe it can be resuscitated."

Melanie decided to grab a bite before going home. She walked to a diner around the corner that was popular with hospital employees. It would be deserted at this time, but she knew she could get a decent sandwich there. She ate a hamburger, and called a cab. It arrived in a few minutes, and she gave the driver her address. She was tired, and looked forward to a good night's sleep.

The hall in her building was dim. As she walked toward her apartment, Melanie noticed a sliver of light under the door. Did I leave a light on, she wondered? Gosh, I'm getting as absent minded as Aunt Jody. She turned the key and went inside, then gasped and threw up her hands. Fear enveloped her as she took in the mess that met her eyes. Her apartment had been torn apart. Every drawer was open. Clothes were strewn everywhere, and books and CDs lay on the floor. She screamed, and backed out into the hall. Curiosity finally overcame her.

As she walked tentatively back inside, she felt a dull thud, and suddenly everything went black.

Melanie came too with an excruciating headache. She felt a huge lump on her head, and couldn't move her left leg without a great deal of pain. She dragged herself to the phone and dialed 911, but passed out before she could give any information. When the paramedics arrived, the landlady let them in. She had already called the police. The paramedics secured Melanie to a gurney and stabilized her head, than took her to the hospital. Melanie remained out until the broken bone had been set, and the pain medicine had taken effect. She wanted to sleep, but the nurses kept waking her, suspecting she had a concussion. When they finally let her sleep, her rest was disturbed by nightmares of Matt conking her on the head, and leaving her to die in her apartment.

A crime scene investigator arrived just as the ambulance pulled out of the driveway. He fingerprinted and tagged everything that might be evidence, and outlined the spot where Melanie had fallen. A green suit was laid out on the bed with a Nordstrom's price tag still on it. The receipt was on top of the jacket. Closer examination revealed some words scribbled across the receipt: "I'll bet this is pretty on you." The CSI added the receipt to the bag of evidence. He made a note to get a list of missing items from Melanie when she came home. As he was leaving, he noticed a black address book with some pages torn out of it. He added it to the evidence already collected, then headed for the hospital to get a statement.

They kept Melanie in the hospital for a day and half to monitor her concussion and cast her broken leg. The police grilled her about what had happened. She told the detectives about her past relationship with Matt, and his breaking into the cabin and stealing the gun. But she couldn't give any details about being accosted, except for what she saw in her apartment before someone knocked her cold. When the doctor released her, Rhonda picked her up. Melanie filled her in on what had happened, and told her how she'd met Dwayne. Rhonda was wide eyed as she listened to the story of their whirlwind romance, and the close relationship that had developed so quickly between them. "I'm really happy for you Melanie, but I hate to lose such a good friend and neighbor. I'll really miss you."

"I'll miss you too. We've had some good times, and some good talks."

Rhonda helped Melanie put her apartment back together. Melanie wasn't used to crutches. She stumbled from desk to dresser, discovering things that were missing. She stopped in front of a glass cabinet. "Hey, my Lladros are gone, and my crystal cats." That bastard, he took everything valuable. I wonder if he took my jewelry!"

Melanie went to the dresser and saw that her jewelry case was almost empty. Matt had left just a few pieces and her watch. He'd also taken several first edition novels that she treasured. He'd taken her camera, but left her computer. Melanie picked up the phone to notify the CSI of the missing items. "You know," she told Rhonda, "most of the things he took were presents he gave me. If the police pick him up, he'll say they were his. You know, I don't even want them now. I don't want anything that reminds me of him. I just want him out of my life."

Rhonda patted Melanie's arm. "I understand, kid. I'd feel the same way. I wonder why he took your things."

"I remember the deputy telling us that, when they stopped Matt for speeding, he was driving a ten-year-old Buick, so he must have been broke. And if he was doing drugs again …" It was all beginning to make sense. Melanie shivered at the thought of her precious things in a pawnshop, and Matt using the money to buy drugs. "Thanks for all your help Rhonda. Say, the suite at the ranch where we'll be living is completely furnished. I'm just taking a few of my favorite pieces. Are you interested in buying my furniture? I'll give you a good price, than you can rent the place out furnished."

"You bet. I've always loved your furniture." Rhonda looked around and smiled. "You know what? I'm going to put most of it into my own apartment. I'll give the new tenant my old stuff. I'll wave some burning sage around this place to erase the bad vibes."

Melanie laughed and gave Rhonda a hug. "Good idea. Thanks again."

After Rhonda left, Melanie sat for a long time, lost in thought. She finally picked up her cell phone and called Izzy. The call went to the answering machine. "Hi Izzy. Gee, I really need to talk to you. I just got home from the hospital. Someone broke into my apartment and stole a lot of my things. I think it was Matt. I got bopped on the head and I have a concussion. My leg is broken and it's in a cast. I'll be here for a while, than I'm going to Rhonda's, so call me on my cell."

The next call was to the massage studio. Sara was at the front desk and was surprised to hear from her. "Girlfriend! I didn't expect a call from you so soon. Paula, pick up the other phone, Melanie's on the line. What have you been up to? And what's all this mystery stuff you were going to tell us?"

"I have lots of good news and some bad news." She described the ranch, and Dwayne and his family.

"A cowboy dude? What about Matt? Weren't you going to meet him at the farmers market?"

Melanie sighed and told them everything that had happened, ending with the two break-ins. Sara and Paula's faces were grim as she told them about the missing gun and the valuables he'd taken from her apartment. "But it gets worse. Would you believe, he followed me here, conked me on the head, and left me for dead! I have a broken leg from the fall, and a slight concussion. Sheesh—you never really know a guy do you."

"That S.O.B. Mel, are you hurt bad? Are you going to press charges? Do you think you'll ever get your stuff back?"

Melanie told them what she'd told Rhonda. "My head hurts, and my leg's in a cast, but that will heal. All I want is to pack up my things and get back to Dwayne. I've given notice at the hospital, and to Rhonda. She's buying my furniture. Hey kids, this means I won't be working with you any more."

Sara and Paula's faces fell as they absorbed what Melanie was saying. "So you're going to live up there at the ranch. That sucks. For us I mean. But good for you girlfriend. Hey, Melanie, do you love him?"

Melanie's eyes sparkled. "I love him, and I like him, and he's the sexiest hunk I ever laid eyes on. I can't keep my paws off him. He has a great sense of humor. I've had more fun with Dwayne than I ever did with Matt, even in the good days before he started drinking. And I love Dwayne's family and the ranch. It's so different from city life."

Sara and Paula's faces lit up. "Well, that's great." Sara said. "And hey, don't worry about us, we'll find someone to fill your spot." She screwed up her face, not sure just how easy that was going to be. "So you go for it girl. "Mel, do you need anything? Paula can cover here for a couple of days if you want me to come over and help you."

"Thanks. You're a doll for asking. Rhonda wants me to stay with her, so I'll be well taken care of. I love ya both."

Melanie called Dwayne and told him what happened. He immediately jumped in the truck, leaving the ranch chores to the hands. He broke all speed limits, and arrived in record time. When he knocked on the door of the apartment, Rhonda let him in and introduced herself. Melanie was leaning on the counter, talking on her cell phone. She was on crutches, and was still pretty wobbly. She looked like she'd seen a ghost. When she saw Dwayne, she ended the conversation, set down the phone, and fell into his arms. He held her tenderly and she cried and cried. The story was told and retold, along with the news she'd just heard on the phone.

"Nettie was asked to work late. After her shift she went into the locker room to change. A male nurse, one of the layoffs, grabbed her and ran a knife into her, right between her ribs. Fortunately, the knife missed Nettie's organs, but he also broke her right arm and two fingers on her left hand when she tried to get away. Nettie said the man was completely out of control. He ranted that all the women got to keep their jobs and got all the overtime, while the men got laid off. He said he was going to fix Nettie so she'd never work again, then maybe they'd give him his job back. Nettie said when he finally let her go, there was blood everywhere. An intern heard him yelling and looked in. When he saw what was happening, he called the emergency room and the police."

"And here's the last straw. Nettie can't find anyone to help her. All her friends and neighbors work. Her sister wouldn't come unless she could bring her boyfriend, and Nettie said that was out of the question. Disability will pay her medical expenses, but won't pay for home care. Moesha is determined to quit school and stay home to take care of her aunt. Nettie said she was adamant about her intention, and didn't think she could change her mind. She said Moesha is already looking for a part-time job to help pay the bills." Melanie was beside herself. "This is too much. These are good people. Why is this happening to them, and to me, while Matt gets away with my belongings to buy drugs?" Dwayne and Rhonda nodded agreement. Melanie suddenly brightened. "Dwayne, this is what I'm going to do. I'm going to take care of them until Nettie is able to be on her own. With both hands out of commission, and the abdominal wound, she's going to need help for a couple of weeks. As soon as she's back on her feet, I'll come back to the ranch. By then, everything will be back to normal. What do you think?"

Dwayne's face showed exactly what he thought. "No way. You are coming home with me so I can take care of you. Nettie can hire someone to help her so Moesha can graduate. You, my sweet, are in no position to care for someone else, nurse or not. It will be hard to get around on crutches, and it'll be weeks until that bone heals. Melanie please listen. Come back with me today. You'll be swarmed with attention at the ranch. Remember how they smothered Ida?"

Melanie laughed. "It's tempting, but Dwayne, I feel I owe something to Nettie. I don't know why. I think it's that I know she'd do the same for me if she were in my place."

Dwayne used every method of persuasion he could think of. He finally realized there was no changing Melanie's mind. Like his mother, she would stick to her plan, even if it wasn't in her best interest. But deep down, he knew she was doing the right thing for her new friend, and admired her for her spunk. He also knew enough about broken bones from his own experience to know her leg would heal quickly. But that wasn't the answer he wanted. He already missed Mel, and wanted her at his side every moment. Life was drab with her away, and he'd felt himself slipping back into the blue state he'd dropped into after Cindy died. He suddenly snapped out of it. What's the matter with me, he thought. Here I am feeling sorry for myself when all this garbage is being dumped on Melanie and her friend. "Okay sweet lady, go do your thing. But be careful, and please hire some help so you can both heal as quickly as possible. Then come home to me. I love you, and I want us to be together."

Melanie hugged Dwayne. "I knew you'd understand. I love you too, and I'll miss you. But it'll only be for a couple of weeks, and it will make a big difference in Nettie's and Moesha's lives."

Dwayne packed up a few of the items Melanie wanted to bring back to the ranch. He knew the situation was temporary, but he was very unhappy that their life together would be on hold for a while.

Melanie slept fitfully. Her leg ached. Every time she turned over, it went into an awkward position, and the cast weighed a ton. She woke up with a throbbing headache where the bluish lump on her head was. The next morning she called Izzy and left another message on her cell phone. "Hey Kiddo, call me, okay. I really need to talk to you. My plans have changed for a while. I'm moving in with a family that needs help, and I need to tell you what's been happening here."

Then she called the ranch. "Hi Hilda, it's Melanie. Did Dwayne get home okay?"

"Yes, he and Jody are with the vet taking care of Anabelle. She delivered the twins this morning. It was a hard birth. The calves are doing fine now. They're both on their feet and wanting to nurse, but Anabelle retained one of the placentas. The vet's working to expel it so she won't get an infection. They're so cute. One's a heifer and the other's a bull. They both have Anabelle's markings."

"Wow, I can't wait to see them. I have a new horror story about Matt, and my friend at the hospital was attacked too, but I'm sure Dwayne brought you all up to date on that."

"Yes. Dwayne told us what happened to you and Nettie. He assured us that you were well enough to take care of your friend. But he sure isn't happy about your being apart for a while."

"I know. I'll miss him too, but the time will pass quickly. Say, did the coyote come back?"

Hilda laughed. "He sure did. We heard a whole pack howling around sundown in the woods in back of cabin nine. Wait 'til you hear what the guys did. Dwayne, Marcus, Lance, and a couple of the other ranch hands each drank as much of a six-pack as they could with the idea of doing some marking of their own. You should have seen them. They could hardly walk. Their stomachs were jiggling and gurgling." Melanie could hear Luz laughing in the background. "They managed to get down to the woods though, and peed on everything in sight. We hope that did the trick because, when they got back, they were all sick. They swore never to do anything like that again. None of them are big drinkers."

Melanie laughed as she visualized the men lurching around the woods with their flies open. "What a sight that must have been. Too bad Tom had to miss that. How's Ida?"

"She's doing much better. The doctor is going to release her tomorrow. They'll be back around three. None too soon either. She says it's like being in jail. You can't do this, and you can't do that, and its poke and prod all day and all night. She said she hasn't had a wink of sleep, or anything fit to eat the whole time."

Melanie laughed. "I think she's exaggerating a little. Tell Dwayne not to worry, and that I love him."

"Bless you child, I'll tell him. He sets a store on you, too. And bless you again for taking care of your friends. As much as I want to see you back here with Dwayne, I know that you are doing the right thing, as they would have done for you. Dwayne sure misses you when you're away though. He loves you very much."

"I miss him too. I hope to be back soon. Bye."

Melanie hung up, and saw there was a message on her cell phone from Izzy. "Hi Mel. I just got your message. My gosh, are you okay? We keep missing each other. I'm on the road too, but if you need help, I'll come and stay with you for a while. Bruce is taking me to meet his mother. He's really smitten. I like him, but I wish he'd slow down a little. Hey, here he comes. I'll try you again later." Melanie called her back, but got a recorded message that the number she was dialing was out of her calling area. "Darn, this is so frustrating."

Chapter 17 – Twins

The vet left at 6:30. Dwayne and Jody came back to the house famished, and devoured the dinner Luz set out for them. Hilda told Dwayne about Melanie's call, and he said he'd call her back after dinner. Jody brought everyone up to date on Anabelle. "She finally expelled the placenta. The vet said she should be okay now, but we've got to watch and make sure the little one gets enough milk. The bull's much bigger than the heifer, and he's already more aggressive. We'll have to keep an eye on Gracie for a while. We named them George and Gracie."

Hilda mentioned that she told Melanie what had happened with the coyotes. Dwayne howled, "aauuwooo," and Goldie looked this way and that, her tail pointed for the hunt. Dwayne called her. "Come here, girl," he said. "That was just me, howling at the moon. I think our antics finally got rid of the coyotes for good. Whew, that was a night we're not likely to forget."

Tom brought Ida home the next day. When Dwayne told his parents everything that had happened they were amazed, and very concerned about Melanie. Dwayne called her, and put Tom on the line. Melanie told him she was doing much better. "The doctor said there's no danger from the concussion, and I still have all my marbles. My leg slows me up though. It's awkward to get around with this cast, but it's doable. I'm far better off than Nettie, and I really want to help her get through this."

Tom could hear the same determination in Melanie as he saw in Ida when she set her mind to doing something. "Okay, if you're sure it's not going to put you back any. But if you get to feeling bad, or need help with anything, you call us."

Tom handed the phone back to Dwayne. "Mel, we all care about you, I hope Nettie heals fast so you can come home soon." Dwayne told her the details about the calves' births.

"George and Gracie! I love it. Those names are perfect. I can't wait to see them. Rhonda's going to drive me to Nettie's tonight. I'll get a better idea of what's going on when I see her."

"Okay. Take care of yourself, and keep in touch. I love you."

Dwayne put one arm around Ida and one around his father. "Boy, its sure great to have you home. The staff has seen to things around the ranch, and no problems have come up. But wait until I tell you what we did with the coyotes." Dwayne related the story in such detail that Tom and Ida could visualize the men staggering around the woods. Ida clapped her hands together, and Tom tipped his head back. They both laughed, and Dwayne joined them.

Dwayne took Tom up to see the calves. Tom kneeled down and touched them all over, as if to assure that every bone and muscle was in its place. He patted Anabelles head. "Good going, girl. Those are two fine specimens you produced. You should be proud." Gracie nuzzled Anabelle and latched onto a nipple. After a few minutes, George joined her, and insisted on grabbing the same nipple, nudging Gracie, and blocking her so she couldn't nurse. Tom led Anabelle a few feet away and Dwayne grabbed George around the neck. He protested at first, but gave in when he felt Dwayne scratching behind his ears. "I think we're going to have trouble with this guy. He wants those udders all to himself. He's a typical bull, territorial and hungry, and mighty persistent. We'll have to watch Gracie to make sure she gains weight. How're those kittens doing?

Dwayne smiled. "They're cute as the dickens. Their main interest is still their mom's belly, but they're becoming more aware of what's going on around them now, and will pounce on anything that moves. Come on, let's go see them." The kittens were asleep in a heap on the hay. They were all tangled together so you couldn't tell whose paw or tail belonged to whom. Tiger sat guard in a corner, and came over with a "meow" to greet them.

Dwayne rinsed out Tiger's water dish and filled it with fresh water. He poured some kibble into her bowl, and Tiger padded over to test it out. Tasting the same old fare, she put her tail in the air, indicating her lack of interest, and went over to the kittens. She picked one up by the scruff of the neck and brought it over to her corner, then proceeded to lick it from top to bottom. The other kittens woke up and untangled themselves. One by one they stretched and arched their backs, then looked around to see what mischief they could get into. Tom picked up the orange one. "This one's a cutie pie. Look at those green eyes. They almost sparkle. Ida's going to get a kick out of them. I'll bring her up tomorrow when she's had a chance to rest up a bit. I think she's lost some strength from being off her feet for so long. Doc Elmer said she should take it easy for a while. She hasn't lost her spunk, though. She sure gave that nurse what for. We met up with her in the hall when we were leaving. Ida wagged her finger at her and told her she'd better go get her glasses checked before she gave someone the wrong medicine and caused some real problems. The nurse put her head down and mumbled an apology, than slunk away." Tom laughed. "She's a strong woman, she is. Over the years we've been married, I've found it's best to stay on her good side."

Chapter 18 – Nettie

At first Nettie wouldn't hear of Melanie coming to help her when she had injuries of her own to heal, but after much persuasion, she gave in. Melanie could almost hear the relief in her new friend's voice. "I'll tell Moesha when she gets home. Would you believe, she's already applied for several jobs!"

Nettie couldn't drive, so hadn't returned for her follow-up appointment. She told Melanie she suspected the wound had become infected. She was running a fever, and was dehydrated. Melanie called a cab and brought her back to the emergency room. They cleaned and dressed her wound, and she was put on an I.V. of antibiotics and fluids. The doctor was reluctant to release her right away, so they kept her another day.

Melanie called the local market and had food delivered, mostly ready-to-eat dinners since she was still clumsy getting around on the crutches. She and Moesha fixed up a place for Nettie on the sofa so they could keep an eye on her. Moesha rushed home from school every afternoon. She waited on her aunt hand and foot, so Melanie was able to rest her leg in the afternoon. Moesha hated the TV dinners, and begged her aunt to let her learn to cook. She was soon able to set out a pretty good dinner, and was very proud of her new accomplishment.

Nettie and Melanie exchanged stories about their lives. They marveled that such a bizarre set of circumstances had to happen for them to meet, being they'd been working in the same hospital for many years. Moesha told her story too, causing tears all around. Nettie vowed she would never allow her niece to return to her mother as long as her boyfriend lived there. She had suspected for a long time that things were not right in her sister's household, but she had no idea that

Moesha was being molested. She took great pains to assure Moesha that none of this was her fault. She told her she had done right thing, fending Duke off all those years, and begging her mother to send him away. Nettie thought to herself how lucky it was that things hadn't gotten even more out of hand. She was glad her sister finally decided to send her daughter away. She'd been horrified when she said she would come to help only if she could bring her boyfriend. "Lord, sometimes my sister doesn't seem to have good sense. I'm going to give her a piece of my mind when I'm back on my feet."

Dwayne called Melanie every night to tell her what was happening at the ranch, and to make sure she was able to handle Nettie's needs without re-injuring her leg. Melanie told him that Moesha had taken over the cooking and cleaning, and assured him that the light nursing Nettie needed was easy for her to do, even with her gimpy leg, Time passed quickly, and after a week, Dwayne reported that Sharon had called. Melanie's theory about Jeff was right on. Knowing how much Sharon missed riding, he'd found an academy and signed up for riding lessons on Tuesdays and Thursdays. On Sharon's birthday, she found his certificate of completion tucked into her birthday card, along with a twelve-month pass for two at the stables. "Sharon is so happy, and said to thank you for saving her from confronting Jeff and stirring things up over nothing. She said she'll probably tell him what she was thinking some day, but doesn't want to ruin all the good feelings right now."

Melanie tried to jump up and down, but couldn't get very far on one foot. "I'm so happy to hear that. I've been thinking about Sharon, and hoping things would work out for her. "

After a couple of weeks, Nettie was strong enough to take over some of the household chores. When Melanie was sure she and Moesha would be okay on their own, she called Dwayne and told him she was ready to come home. He was delighted, and arranged to pick her up the next day. Melanie exchanged tearful goodbyes with her friends, and they thanked her for all she had done. "Now you be good to that girl," Nettie told Dwayne. "She's surely an angel."

Part IV

Chapter 19 – Home

Dwayne and Melanie drove straight through to the ranch. When they arrived, it was late, and the rest of the household were asleep. Dwayne brought Melanie's things in, and helped her put her clothes away. Melanie yawned and flopped down on the bed. "This feels so good. I could sleep for a week." She turned onto her side and stretched, then remembered the nightmare she'd had on the train.

Dwayne saw her face change. "What is it Mel? What's wrong?"

She told him the about the dream. "It seemed so real. I could feel his hand tightening around my throat. Moesha woke me. I had cried out loud in my sleep. I thought that Matt had grabbed my arm, but it was Moesha, shaking my arm to wake me up. I'm going to keep in touch with them. I'm so glad Moesha got away from her mother's boyfriend. She was kind to me, and spoke with great insight, although she's only fifteen. She thought you were the one in my nightmare. She lectured me about staying with someone who—how did she put it— something like, 'when a man's no good, he never does get any better, and sooner or later you're gonna get hurt.'"

Dwayne nodded. "Those are words of wisdom, spoken, unfortunately, by a child with experience. I'll bet she's told that same thing to her mother. They sound like good people. We should invite them for a visit some time." Dwayne sat down next to Melanie and put his arm around her. "I'm so sorry Matt turned out to be such a jerk. Are you sure you don't want to press charges?"

Melanie shook her head. "I've thought about it, and I'm pretty sure what he did was done under the influence of alcohol or drugs. Another stint in jail won't help him. What he needs is to get into a program to get clean and sober. As long as he stays away from us, I want to just let it go."

Dwayne yawned. "Okay, if you're sure. I'll talk to Dad and see what he wants to do about the gun. Well, I'm ready for bed. We've both had a long day." Melanie nodded, and they washed up and slipped under the covers. Melanie fell asleep immediately, but Dwayne lay awake for a while, musing over the things she'd told him about Matt. He was pretty sure they'd seen the last of him, but he was still worried that it hadn't all been resolved. And Matt still had the gun. Was he planning to sell it? Or use it to rob someone? Or, was he planning to come after Melanie or him? He finally managed to put everything out of his mind, and fell asleep.

The next morning Melanie saw that Dwayne had drawn a red heart on her cast, with "Dwayne + Melanie" carefully lettered in the center of it. Over the next few days, the rest of the family and staff added their good wishes and autographs. Jody added a Goldie-sized footprint, four cat paws, and a cowbell. The cast became a work of art, and a statement of the love the family felt for Melanie.

Melanie kept trying to reach Izzy, but kept getting the same annoying message on her machine: "Hello, this is Izzy, please leave a message."

"Hi Izzy, it's me again. I'm dying to hear what's going on with you and Bruce. So you're meeting his mother? Sounds like you work as fast as I do. I have some really big news too, but I don't want to tell it to you through this moron answering machine. Call me as soon as you can. I'm going to drag my cell phone around until I hear from you. Hope you're having fun. Bye."

Melanie's walking cast slowed her down, but she managed to wobble around the ranch. She was entranced with the woodshop. She'd done some wood carving in college, but had never seen raw wood made into such fine furniture. All the pieces had "Bar None" carved into them, and were carefully made out of the finest grained hardwood, with tongue and groove joints.

Dwayne did the rounds on his own, since Melanie's cast prevented her from riding. Most of the cabins were already vacated. School would start soon, and there was always a lull before the holidays. Reservations had already started to come in for Thanksgiving, and they always had a full house for Christmas.

Melanie managed to limp up the hill to see the kittens. They wrestled and pounced and tumbled over each other. She sat on a stool and called "here kitty." The kittens looked up, and the orange one padded over. Melanie took her on her lap, and petted her soft fur. She was her favorite too, with her four white paws and white face. She climbed up on her shoulder and purred contentedly. Melanie ended up at Anabelle's pen and Dwayne rode up just as she arrived. The calves were adorable. Gracie was underweight, which was normal for a twin. She was standing by, watching pudgy George greedily sucking away. As Melanie and Dwayne watched, Anabelle nudged George, and broke away from him. She went over to Gracie, but George bullied his way over again.

Dwayne threw up his hands. "This is no good. We've got to divert George so Gracie can nurse. I'm going to organize a chain watch. We'll arrange to have someone here supervising every couple of hours until that little one gains some weight. I'll make up a schedule."

He found a rope and tied it loosely around the bull's head. George fought it for a minute, than gave in and let Dwayne lead him away from Anabelle. Gracie went over to nurse. When she had her fill, they untied George. He went right for Anabelle and began sucking again. Dwayne and Melanie laughed. "We'll have to figure out what to do with him when he's full grown. He's going to be a real handful." They went back to the house. Dwayne made up the schedule, and passed out copies to the ranch hands. Everyone was happy to take a couple of shifts each day.

Time seemed to stand still for Melanie. The cast became an enemy, impeding all the activities she loved. She couldn't get it wet, so couldn't swim or use the hot tub. She couldn't ride, or play tennis, or square dance. Even walking was painfully slow. She and Dwayne had done no more than hold and kiss each other, and their need to be together was becoming urgent. To add insult to injury, the skin under the cast itched like crazy, and she couldn't reach the places that needed scratching the most. Finally the time was up, and Melanie made an appointment with Dr. Elmer to have the cast removed. Her nerves fluttered as she watched the saw cut through, close to the skin. The doctor teased that he hadn't cut a cast off since Dwayne's broken leg when he was a kid. "Now hold still little lady. Dwayne, you'd better go around and give her a bear hug from the back. Hold her tight so she can't move."

Dwayne beamed. "There's nothing I'd rather do." The doctor smiled, glad to see Dwayne so happy after all the pain he'd suffered with his wife's illness and death.

The cast finally separated, and the doctor pried it open and slipped it off. "Oh no—my poor leg!" Melanie was aghast at the sight of her white limb. It was atrophied and wrinkled and ugly. She had seen this happen to numerous patients, but was not prepared for it to happen to her.

"Don't worry, all it needs is some exercise and a little sun and it'll catch up. Here are some physical therapy exercises to do every day, and try to walk as much as possible. No running yet, or tennis, but swimming is good. Wait another few weeks to get your strength back, than you can try getting on a horse. But don't do it alone. You're likely to be a little stiff for a while, and I don't want you taking a tumble before that bone is completely knit."

Melanie had to force herself to slow down. She was used to a fast pace, and caught herself rushing here and there. She took long walks around the ranch, and was diligent about doing the physical therapy. Her strength improved each day. After a couple of weeks, she was able to walk the entire ranch in the morning, and swim late in the evening. All the exercise sent her to bed early, and she finally caught up on her sleep. It was so nice not to have that monster attached to her leg.

Chapter 20 – Engaged

The alarm clock in Dwayne's head rang at six. He crept out of bed, being careful not to disturb Melanie. He shaved, then filled the bathtub with hot water and started the bubbles and water jets. Melanie heard the racket, and came in to see what was going on. "I'm going to take a bath. Want to join me?"

"Mmm, sounds great, just a minute." She came back in her bathrobe and gave him a kiss. Dwayne picked her up, and pretended to toss her in the tub fully dressed. "Hey, put me down. Help!"

"Shhh," cried Dwayne. "You'll have the whole family back here." He quieted her with a kiss, than put her down. "So you'd rather skinny dip, huh. Here, I can help with that." He took off her robe and tossed it aside. He gently pushed her straps down, and her gown dropped to the floor. He drew her to him and whispered, "You are so beautiful, you take my breath away."

"Whoa, and you—you're already wide awake." Melanie laughed as she saw Dwayne spring to life under his shorts. She kissed him, feeling a hot tingle spread throughout her whole body. Dwayne dropped his shorts and kicked them the rest of the way off, then picked her up again and carried her into the bathtub.

They soaped each other up, and let the water jets rinse and soothe them. Dwayne edged around Melanie and sat down behind her. She snuggled close, and his arms crept around her. He touched her softly all over, the way she'd always dreamed of being touched. "You are so wonderful" he whispered. "I will love you all the rest of my days. I missed you so much when you were away."

"I missed you too. I love you too, Dwayne, and I want so much for us to be together. But part of me wants to wait. It's that old practical side of me that's always horning in on my good times." Melanie giggled. "Oops, that was a poor choice of words."

"I think that word was very appropriate." Dwayne threw his head back and laughed, then turned serious. "I want you too, but I understand how you feel. I'm very sure that I want you in my life permanently, but we've only known each other a short time, and part of that time we've been apart. Let's give it a couple more days."

Melanie caught the word "days." She turned to face Dwayne, intending to correct him, but saw that his eyes were crinkled up and there was a mischievous grin on his face.

"Oh you, I was all ready to give you another lecture." Dwayne laughed and Melanie joined in. They sat in the tub for a long time, making plans and dreaming of what was to be.

Melanie finally got up. "Time to get out, I'm getting cold." She grabbed a towel and handed it to Dwayne, then took one for herself.

They got dressed and sat down on the bed. Dwayne took Melanie's hand. "We never talked about having children. Do you want to have kids?"

"I do. I've been thinking about that since we saw the babies in the maternity ward. How about you, do you still want to have kids, being you're so old?" Melanie teased.

Dwayne scowled. "Old? I'm still a teenager at heart, and I absolutely want us to have children. How many shall we have?"

Melanie smiled. "At least two, a boy and girl."

"Yes! "Our son can look like me, but our daughter's got to have your curly hair and green eyes. Our son and daughter—I love the sound of those words."

Melanie picked up a pillow and cradled it, singing "lullaby, and goodnight." She laid it down on the dresser, and picked up a corner of the pillow case. She made a face and held her nose. "Phew, Dwayne— come here and change this baby's diaper. It's your turn."

Dwayne grabbed the pillow and gave it back to her. "No way, I did it last time." Besides, you get to do the stinky ones."

"Uh uh, we're going to share everything. Melanie picked up the pillow and held it out in front of her. Dwayne grabbed his hat and put it on top. Melanie laughed. "These kids are going to have cowboy hats and boots in their layettes. You'll have them on a horse before they can walk."

"That's the way to go. You've got to start 'em young. We'll have to open a college fund too. They should both go to college, then they can decide what they want to do after they graduate." He grabbed Melanie around the waist and patted her tummy. "You'll look so cute with a belly full of baby."

Melanie laughed. "Cute! I'll look like Anabelle. And wait until they start talking back. I think that starts at two years old, and continues until they're eighteen. Speaking of riding, I think I'm ready to get back on a horse. I'd like to do rounds with you this morning."

Dwayne hugged her. "That's great. I'm so glad to have the whole Melanie back. We'll take it real easy."

After breakfast, they saddled Danny. Dwayne took down the mounting block Melanie used when she first started riding. He helped her mount, urging her to be careful, and to tell him if anything hurt. Melanie said there was no pain, not even a twinge. Dwayne saddled Jenny and they did their morning scout of the ranch, keeping the horses at a slow walk. They ended up at cabin nine. There was no evidence of coyote activity, but when they looked inside the cabin, Melanie felt the same cold prickles down her back. They stayed only a minute, then rode back to the stables.

"Say Mel, I have some business in the jewelry shop in town this afternoon. Do you want to go?" Melanie's sparkling eyes told Dwayne she was already there.

The shop was near the drugstore where they'd had lunch. They looked in the windows. The one on the left had hand-crafted necklaces and bracelets made of jade, leather, and gemstones. Dwayne steered Melanie to the other window where the diamond jewelry was displayed. A collection of engagement and wedding rings was arranged on a slowly-revolving pyramid, covered in black velvet. "This is what I wanted to show you. Which one do you like?"

Melanie caught her breath. "Oh, Dwayne, I feel like Cinderella, they're all so beautiful. But should we—I mean we just—and it's so soon."

Dwayne put his arms around Melanie. "A ring makes it official. Besides, we can't come back ringless. The folks are somewhat old fashioned, and like all the traditions upheld. And for that matter, so do I."

Melanie frowned. "How do you think Tom and Ida feel about your moving into the east wing with me before we're married?"

"Fortunately, Sharon and Jeff cleared the way for us on that one. Sharon met Jeff at Cal State. They lived together for a year on campus. The job Jeff was offered wasn't funded yet. They were engaged, but didn't want to get married until they could afford a place of their own. Sharon asked Mom and Dad if she could bring Jeff home for a while. They said sure, not realizing what she meant. When Jeff brought his bag into Sharon's room, the folks were mighty upset. Sharon argued that it was the ninety's, and everybody did it. She finally told them they'd already been living together for a year, and that won them over. Jody was on their side from the beginning. She's got a good head on her. She isn't influenced by things like outdated traditions, or what the neighbors will say, so we're not likely to get any flack from her."

Melanie smiled. "That's a relief. I've been worried about that."

Dwayne took Melanie's hand and led her into the shop. A smiling salesman greeted them. "Howdy folks. I'm Lester Manning. How can I help you today?"

Dwayne pointed to the window display. "We'd like to look at some engagement rings." Lester's smile stretched from ear to ear. Dwayne asked a lot of questions about the rings' gold content, and the diamonds' cut, sparkle and clarity, qualities that Melanie hadn't even known diamonds possessed. She tried on several styles, and chose the one she liked best.

Lester measured her finger, and took the ring back to the technician to be sized. He brought back a kit with a soft brush and some jewelry cleaner, and showed Melanie how to clean the ring and buff it to bring out the shine. "Now don't be afraid to wear it. Diamonds are hard, and are meant to be worn every day. Just check it every now and then to be sure the setting is secure. How would you like to pay for that sir?"

Dwayne took out a credit card, and Lester wrote up the sale. He put the cleaning kit in a bag with the receipt. The technician brought the ring back, tucked into a tiny velvet box lined with white satin. Dwayne took it and placed it ceremoniously on Melanie's finger. "Now we're officially engaged." He kissed her fingertips.

Lester and the tech clapped. "You folks have made my day. Have you set a wedding date yet?"

"That's the next thing on our agenda. Thanks for all your help." They shook hands all around, and Melanie and Dwayne left hand in hand.

Melanie danced around Dwayne. "This is the happiest day of my life. Will you always be this good to me?" She answered her own question. "Never mind, I know you will be."

Dwayne took her hand. "You have my pledge, Mel. I love you very much."

Chapter 21 – Sad News

Melanie and Dwayne got in late. Melanie had fallen asleep on the way back, and when then got home, they went right to bed. They were awakened the next morning by Dwayne's cell phone. "Hello," he said sleepily.

There was a crackle, than a voice said, "Hello Dwayne, this is Craig Benson. Remember me, Matt Walters' friend?"

Dwayne was instantly awake. When he heard Matt's name, his stomach knotted. "Hello Craig. It's been a long time, but of course I remember you. What can I do for you?"

"I'm sorry to bother you so early in the morning, but I'm hoping you can help me out. Matt's mother died yesterday. I've been trying to reach Matt to tell him. I can't find him anywhere, and he doesn't answer his phone. Do you know where he is, or how to contact him?"

"I'm so sorry to hear that. What happened?"

"She had a heart attack. They did everything they could but, well, she's gone."

Dwayne told Craig to hold the line for a minute. He held his hand over the speaker and relayed the message to Melanie. "I think its okay to tell him what's been going on. He's a playboy, but he has a good heart. He was trying to help Matt, and he seemed to be trustworthy. What do you think?"

Melanie nodded. "I'm sure its okay. Go ahead and tell him."

Dwayne explained what happened with Matt. He told Craig how he'd met Melanie, and that they'd fallen in love, and were planning to be married. He ended with the two break-ins, the assault on Melanie and the missing gun.

"No kidding!" Craig said. "I'm really surprised to hear that. You know, I can't see Matt hitting Melanie, or shooting anyone. But if he needed money, he may have figured the gun was worth something at a pawnshop. If he were drunk or drugged enough, maybe he—hey, I'm not going to tell his family any of this right now. They've got enough to deal with. I'm staying with the old man and the girls for a while. They're falling apart. Matt's father's got a bum leg, and isn't able to get around easily. He hasn't been himself since his wife died. Susan's in school now, but Julie is still a baby. Nancy was taking care of all three of them. She was a wonderful person. The kids loved her. I loved her too, she was like a second mother to me." Craig's voice cracked as he tried to hold back the tears. "I told them I'd stay with them until they could get a nanny or housekeeper. They need to set a date for the funeral, but want to get hold of Matt first."

"Gee, that's tough. I am so sorry." Dwayne sighed. "Is there anything we can do?"

"Do you or Melanie know how to get hold of Matt?" Craig asked.

"He called here a while ago before he broke in, but when I called him back I got his answering machine. I left a message, but he never returned it." Dwayne gave Craig the number.

"That's the same one I have. Well if you hear from him, tell him he can reach me on my cell phone. So he sent you after Melanie, and now you two are together. Funny how things work out. Well, it sounds like he missed the boat. I never met Melanie, but Matt couldn't say enough about her. He talked all the time about cleaning up his act so she'd take him back, but I guess he just couldn't let go of the drugs and booze. Too bad, because he's really a nice guy when he's clean and sober."

Matt frowned. "I know. Hey, let us know if there's anything else we can do, and I'll call you if we hear from Matt. Please relay our sympathy to the family." Dwayne hung up and sat quietly for a minute to digest it all, then filled Melanie in on the rest of the conversation.

Melanie paced up and down as she listened to Dwayne. "I feel so sad for those poor little girls. It's good of Craig to stay with them for a while, but a housekeeper or nanny! That's no way to raise young children."

"I know, but Craig says their grandfather isn't able to take care of them. They don't have any other family either. At least, I don't remember them mentioning any. Let's get dressed and tell the others."

Everyone sat spellbound while Dwayne told about Craig's call. Then they all started talking at once, a routine that Melanie was getting used to. Their comments ranged from sympathy for Craig and the grandfather, to concern for the little girls' welfare. They were furious with Matt for his misdeeds, and for not being available when he was so desperately needed by his family. Tom shook his head, then went to Ida and put his arm around her. "Boy, you never know when something like that's gonna happen. I'm so glad you're okay." He kissed his wife on the cheek and hugged her. "I don't know what I'd do if something like that happened to you."

Ida squeezed his hand. "Don't you worry now. That blood clot taught me a lesson I'm not likely to forget. From now on, I'm taking care of myself, even if it means having to drink some of Luz's green tea now and then."

Tom laughed and kissed Ida on the cheek. "It's good that Craig is taking responsibility, and will make sure the girls will have someone to take care of them. I'd hate to see them separated, or put into foster homes with strangers."

Jody spoke up. "You know, I'd never want to see that happen. If it comes to that, we should take them in. All of us are cleared for foster care from when you had Tommy. Dwayne, you could renew your license, and it would be easy for Melanie to get cleared."

Dwayne was watching Melanie. "But Jody, they're Matt's kids. After all he's done to Mel?"

Melanie put her hands up. "Wait. Let me think about this. Everything is happening so fast!" They were all quiet for a minute.

Melanie looked up. "Okay. It's true that Matt has been horrid and irresponsible, but that shouldn't reflect on his children. They've been raised by loving grandparents, and now they've suddenly had their world torn apart. I never met the children, in fact I didn't even know Matt had kids until Dwayne told me about them, but I agree with Jody. Although they are not kin to us, Matt was a close friend of Dwayne's, and of mine at one time. So we're not strangers, and we would be able to provide a loving home for the children. If it comes to their having to be placed with strangers, I'd rather they live here. We can raise them with our own kids."

Jody went over to Melanie and put her arms around her. "You're a sweetheart, but what's this I hear about kids of your own. And what's that ring on your finger all about? Is that an engagement ring?" With the news from Craig, Dwayne and Melanie had forgotten to tell the family about their engagement.

Everyone gathered around. Melanie showed them the ring, and told about Dwayne's proposal and their trip to the jewelry store. Everyone started talking at once. Hilda, who had been popping in and out of the kitchen, suggested they move to the dining room, and the rest was told over breakfast. Details of the wedding were discussed, and everyone wished the two a life filled with happiness and lots of children. Ida and Tom hugged Dwayne and Melanie, and confessed they'd been hoping for this for a long time.

After breakfast, Jody went back to the subject of Matt and his little girls. "You know, we're really jumping the gun with this. If the grandfather can't take care of the kids, maybe Craig will want to adopt them. After all, he's their godfather. He doesn't have blood rights, but he could apply for custody couldn't he?"

"He could try," Dwayne explained "but unless he's changed his lifestyle, he may not get it. Craig's got a good heart, there's no denying that. But he drinks too much, and he's got a new girlfriend every other Friday. I don't know how he makes it, but he spends money like water. True, he spends a lot of it on those kids, but unless he gets some stability in his life, he may have a hard time convincing a social worker that he can make a proper home for two little girls."

Ida, who had been quietly taking everything in, suddenly spoke up. "Okay, listen up everybody. I have something to say. First off, we've got to put ourselves in the place of those little girls. Their grandmother's gone, and they just got back from her funeral. Their grandfather loves them, but he can't take care of them. Craig moves in and starts trying out nannies and housekeepers—strangers who, after all, are just hired to do a job. What those children need more than someone to dress them, and take them to school, is a stable, loving environment. They need caring folks to hold them, and let them know its all right to cry. The thing is, they need that right now while they're mourning the loss of their grandma. It sounds like Craig means well, but he's got to be working during the day, and it won't be long before he's out partying again at night."

"Now I have an idea. You all tell me what you think. How about inviting Craig, the children, and their grandfather to come here for a spell after the funeral? We won't mention future plans, just ask them to come for a visit. That'll give us a chance to look at what's happening in that family. We can see how the kids are getting on, and how the grandfather and Craig are handling the situation. Meanwhile we can give the girls the extra love and support they'll need right away, instead of turning them over to a string of hired strangers."

Tom jumped up. "Ida, you are so smart! Why, that makes perfect sense. I don't know why I didn't think of it myself. We can put them up in the west wing, since I noticed Dwayne has moved in with Melanie in the east wing." Tom cleared his throat. "That's okay, kids. I understand. I remember what Sharon said when she and Jeff wanted to live together before they got married. 'After all, we're engaged, and it is the 90's.'" Everyone laughed and Melanie blushed.

Hilda, Luz and Marcus brought in the last dishes and sat down with the family. Hilda raised her hand. "Now I have something to say to all of you, and I'm sure I speak for Luz and Marcus too." Everyone grew quiet. "I've worked for you folks for nigh on to thirty years. You are like family to me, and I love every one of you. You are good people. Over the years you have done some wonderful things, but what I've heard you say today just lightens my heart. What you're thinking of doing, taking on those kids and their grandfather in their time of trouble, is a most generous and loving deed. I'm sure the good Lord's looking on all of you with great pleasure this day."

"Thank you, Hilda," Ida said, and the tears in her eyes glistened.

Everyone went off to their chores thinking about the bizarre set of circumstances that caused such an issue to come up with the Hathaway family. They were very excited about Dwayne and Melanie's engagement, and began thinking about the wedding and how all these changes might affect life at the ranch.

Dwayne called Craig and told him about the Hathaways' invitation. "You're kidding!" Craig said, and a little life came into his voice. "That'd be great. But are you sure? The kids are really down, and so is their grandfather."

"We talked it over, and all of us would like you to come. It will be a diversion for the kids, which might be good for them right now. There's a lot to do here. We have a new litter of kittens, and newborn twin calves. There are horses to ride, and a swimming pool. It will get the kids' minds off their grandmother. Will you come?"

"Wait. Hold on a minute. Let me ask the old man." Craig left the line for a minute, than returned. "He said it sounded fine for the kids, but he wanted to stay behind. He said he doesn't want to travel right now."

"That's no good." Dwayne tried to think of some way to convince him to join them. "Tell him it wouldn't be good for him to be separated from the kids right now."

Craig hesitated. "I don't know."

"Come on, tell him. We really want all of you, and it sounds like he needs our support too."

"Okay, I'll tell you what. I'll convince him. I think it would be good for all of us. Hey, thanks Dwayne. You don't know what a relief this is. I was at a loss to know what to do next, and this will give me some time to figure things out."

Dwayne gave Craig directions to the ranch from the airport. "It's still warm here during the day, but its getting pretty chilly in the evening. Bring warm sweatshirts and jackets for the evening. The pool is still heated, so the kids can swim. Bring their favorite dolls or blankets, or whatever kids that age drag around. When is the funeral?"

"We haven't heard from Matt, so we set it for Thursday. We could fly out Saturday if we can get plane reservations. We can rent a car at the airport. I'll let you know when we're going to arrive." Craig's voice sounded much lighter. "Thanks again, Dwayne. Please tell your family how much I appreciate their inviting us. I'll call you tomorrow."

Dwayne hung up. "**Yes!**" he said and did a thumbs up. "They're coming. Craig said he didn't know what to do next, and this will give him a reprieve. They're shooting for arrival on Saturday. I'll clear the rest of my stuff out of my bachelor's quarters. We can put the overflow into that big room next to the east wing."

Melanie hugged Dwayne and went to tell the others. Dwayne hung back for a minute. Although he knew they'd done the right thing, there were still many things about the situation that bothered him. Craig said he was sure Matt wouldn't use the gun, so why did he take it? If Matt had tried to pawn the gun, it would have been traced by its serial number. And Melanie did get conked on the head and left with a broken leg. And, if Matt had come looking for Melanie at the cabin and her apartment, would he come looking for her here too? A trace of fear mixed with jealousy knotted his stomach. Then he shook it off and went to join the others.

The next few days went by in a flurry. Dwayne and Melanie drove back to her apartment, loaded up the rest of her things, and said goodbye to Rhonda. They stopped at the hospital so Melanie could clean out her locker, and bumped into Nettie. Melanie introduced her to Dwayne, and told her they'd gotten engaged. She showed her the ring, and Nettie graciously wished them a happy married life. They told her about the visitors to the ranch.

Nettie suggested they go to the hospital chapel and get some of the booklets written especially for children who'd lost a loved one. "They are beautifully written and illustrated. They address all the things young children are thinking about, but are afraid to express when there is a death in the family. There are also some booklets for adults that talk about the stages of mourning and how to cope. One of the suggestions for young children is to give them a doll that represents the deceased person. That somehow seems to comfort the little ones."

"Nettie, that's a wonderful idea. Thank you so much. We just packed up the dolls my mother left me. None of them resemble a grandmother, but we'll stop at a toy store and see what we can find. How is Moesha doing?"

"She's just fine, and she's been an angel about helping me. She's very smart and has kept her grades up. She's talking about going to nursing school after she graduates."

Dwayne and Melanie smiled at the news. Melanie hugged Nettie and told her to watch the mail for a wedding invitation. "Be sure to save up some vacation time so you can stay at the ranch for a while."

They found the booklets in the chapel, than went to Toys R Us and told the clerk what they were looking for. He led them to a granny doll made of nylon stockings, stuffed with soft cotton. It had a sweet old face and blue eyes. A couple of aisles down they found a panda bear that was big enough to hug. It had chiffon wings and a gold halo. "That's perfect. We'll take them both."

The next stop was the massage studio. Sara and Paula went bonkers when they saw Melanie and Dwayne. "So you're the one who's stealing Mel away from us," cried Paula. She gave Dwayne a lecture on taking good care of Melanie. Meanwhile, Sara, who was standing behind Dwayne, jumped up and down and pantomimed how cute he was, and that she could eat him up. Melanie tried to shush her, but Dwayne turned and saw the tail end, and they all laughed.

Dwayne told them the date of the wedding. "Plan to stay at the ranch a few days if you like. It'll be off season and you can have your choice of cabins."

Sara smiled. "That sounds great. We'll close the studio for a couple of days so we can stay and visit."

Melanie grabbed her friends together in a hug. "That would be great. The wedding is going to be small and casual. Bring jeans so we can go riding."

Paula folded her arms across her chest. "Count me out. I don't do horses unless they're wooden and attached to a merry-go-round!" Everyone laughed.

"We've got to go. We want to get back by dinner. Okay kids, you take care. I love ya." Melanie and Dwayne hugged Sara and Paula and got into the truck. As they left town, Melanie turned to look out the back window. With a touch of nostalgia, she threw a goodbye kiss to the town she'd lived in since she was a teen.

Part V

Chapter 22 – Izzy

Melanie and Dwayne burst into the kitchen waving a piece of paper. "Craig called, they're all coming, the grandfather too. Craig talked him into it. They'll be here tomorrow afternoon. Here's the airline number and time of arrival. They're renting a car at the airport"

Everyone scurried around excitedly, planning how to furnish the rooms they needed to prepare for the visitors. Dwayne and Melanie told about their encounter with Nettie at the hospital, and showed them the doll and teddy bear. Jody inspected the bear. "Good idea, but the wings should go on the grandma. I'll take them off the teddy bear and sew them on the doll. Got to figure out some way of attaching the halo so it looks like its floating. It's got to look right you know." No one refuted her. Jody always knew what was best.

Just then, a stream of curses was heard. Marcus approached the house and burst through the door, soaking wet. Waving his arms and fuming, he told what had happened. "That animal's a devil, he is. He was nursing and wouldn't let Gracie in, so I put the rope around his neck and led him off towards the water trough. He didn't like having his lunch interrupted. He kept pulling on the rope, trying to get back to Annabelle. When that didn't work, he sidled up right next to me and pushed until I was right up against the trough. Then he butted me. I lost my balance and fell in. You know, I could swear that bull was laughing at me."

Everyone laughed, including Marcus. Tom threw his hands up. "He's a feisty one all right. I'm going to ask around and see if I can find someone who wants to buy him. George is going to be nothing but trouble, and the bigger he gets, the more ornery he's gonna get. Maybe someone's got a cow that's lost her calf and is willing to let him nurse. He'll be valuable as a stud when he's mature."

After dinner, Melanie listened to a message from Izzy on her cell phone. "Hi Mel, gosh, I sure need to talk to you. This thing with Bruce is getting weird. His mother told me some disturbing things about him. She said he's been divorced twice, and got disbarred a couple of years ago for doing something illegal during a trial. He's working now for an insurance company. Bruce didn't tell me any of that. He keeps telling me he loves me, and he's pushing me to do things I'm not ready to do yet. He said he was planning to tell me everything. I had to ask him to leave last night. He wanted to stay over. When I said no, he got really mad. I'm going to break it off with him. Call me so we can talk. I need advice. I want to hear your news too." Izzy's voice sounded shaky at the end of the message.

Melanie put down the phone. "Poor Izzy, she thought she'd finally found a nice guy. What a disappointment. It's incredible that with all those phone calls, we've never connected. I'm beginning to think we'll communicate from now on by answering machine only."

"Is Izzy going to be okay?" Dwayne asked.

"I think so. She can hold her own. She's a strong person, physically and mentally. She works out a lot, and plays tennis. In fact, she's the one who taught me how to play. I think her ego has been hurt the most. I'll call her in the morning. I'm way too tired tonight. I'm going to take a shower and climb into bed. Want to join me?"

"You don't have to ask twice." Dwayne took off his shirt, and Melanie ran the shower. They laughed as they rinsed the soap off each other and made a ceremony of thoroughly drying each other all over. They dove under the covers, and their kisses were soft at first, than became deeper. Melanie could feel Dwayne's hardness pressing against her, and she moved so she could get closer to him. "Oh, Mel, I want you so much. I don't know if I can wait until we're married. I may have to start sleeping in the barn 'til then."

Melanie laughed and drew him closer. "I need you too, and I don't want to wait either. It's been torture being so close and only going so far. I want us to make love now. After all, we're engaged."

Dwayne laughed. He slowly coaxed the straps of Melanie's nightgown off her shoulders and down her arms. Melanie tried to take down Dwayne's shorts, but they caught on his erection. They both giggled as they maneuvered them off. Dwayne pulled her panties down past her soft downy place, and Melanie kicked them off. He caressed her breasts, then moved his hand down to explore further. He trailed his other hand down her back and cupped her round bottom, then explored her softly in places she'd only dreamed of being touched.

Melanie felt a hot tingling flow through her whole body. She moved closer to him and caressed him softly, than kissed him all over. Dwayne moaned. "Melanie, you are the sweetest thing. I love you so much"

Melanie sighed. "I love you too." They moved slowly at first, than their passion erupted into fire, until they reached a peak of ecstasy neither of them had experienced before. When they were satiated, they lay in each others arms for a long time until they finally fell asleep.

Melanie woke up early the next morning. She threw the covers off her, and realized she was naked, than blushed, remembering their lovemaking the night before. She used the bathroom, than carefully climbed back under the covers. Dwayne was on his side facing away from her. She softly kissed his neck, and planted kisses all over his back. Dwayne stirred, and Melanie reached around him to caress his chest. Dwayne turned to her. He kissed her, and gently brushed his hand over her breasts, feeling her nipples came alive in his hand. A sensual heat overcame them and she threw off the covers. Melanie moved her hand down to touch him as they pressed against each other. She felt a hunger she'd never felt before. They kissed and touched and petted each other until neither could wait any longer. Dwayne slowly entered her, and moved gently inside of her. He reached up with one hand and stroked her breasts, and her nipples danced excitedly in his hand. His hand crept down to her downy softness and found her pleasure spot. Melanie threw her head back, arched her back and cried out in delight. They climaxed together, than held each other close for a long time.

Dwayne and Melanie missed breakfast that morning. Although their places at the table were conspicuously empty, no one said a word. They came out of the east wing a little after ten, and Melanie scrambled some eggs and toasted some English muffins. They brought them, and two mugs of coffee back to the east wing to eat, unwilling to let go of the intimacy they had shared.

Later in the day they did the rounds on Jenny and Danny. They unloaded the truck, putting the boxes in the extra room to be unpacked later. Marcus and Tom had moved some furniture out of a bedroom in the west wing. They replaced it with twin beds, nightstands, and a double dresser for the girls. Hilda put up some pretty pink curtains. They added a rocking chair upholstered in pink and white checks and brought out Sharon's old toy box full of toys. It had been stored away in hopes that one day it could be given to a grandchild. Ida looked through her quilts. She found a white one with pink hearts, and one with blue cornflowers that fit the beds. Two old-fashioned doll lamps with ruffled shades from Sharon's room finished it off. The dolls wore pink satin Cinderella gowns, with bonnets to match. They propped the teddy bear on one pillow, and the grandma doll on the other. True to her word, Ida had attached the halo to the doll with fine wire, so it appeared to be floating above her head. The wire was almost invisible.

They planned to put Craig in the guestroom that was furnished with a bed and dresser. Two floor-to-ceiling bookshelves held an extensive library of books ranging from classics to children's stories. They left the bedroom Dwayne had been using intact for Mr. Walters.

Luz was cooking up a storm, and the house smelled delicious. She'd baked batches of chocolate chip and oatmeal cookies. Dwayne sat down at the kitchen table and snatched a handful, and a glass of milk. Luz sat down across from him. "I'm so happy those young ones and their grandfather are coming to stay for a while. In the Philippines, families always stay together and live at home, even when the kids get married. When their parents get old, they stay in the family home and the children take care of them. There's no such thing as an old people's home there."

Dwayne nodded and took another cookie. "That's the way it should be. I'm excited too, but a little nervous. I haven't seen Craig for years, and I don't know what he's like any more. And it's been a while since we had a little one running around the house."

"I know," Luz reminisced. "Fixing up the rooms and putting out the toy box reminded me of Tommy too. I miss him. He was such a happy kid. It'll be different with the little girls. They're likely to be sad and scared, especially at first, but I'm sure they'll brighten up when they see all that's going on here."

Dwayne went to look for Melanie. She had Izzy on her cell phone, and motioned to Dwayne to stay. She looked concerned as she listened to her friend talk. "But Izzy, if you said no, and he tore your clothes off, that's rape!" She listened for a minute. "All right, attempted rape, you should still call the police. Otherwise he may try it again." There was another pause. "Okay, promise? Call them right now. Hey, Izzy, why don't you stay at my apartment for a while. He doesn't know me, so I don't think he could find you there. Rhonda's buying my furniture, so it's still there, and my rent's paid up until the first. You can bring your laptop and work on your book. I'll call Rhonda and tell her you're coming. You can get the key from her. Okay? Good, now call the police. No, not later—right now, okay? All right, call me when you're settled. Bye."

Melanie put the phone down, took a deep breath, and filled Dwayne in on the rest of the conversation. "First of all, Izzy sends us best wishes. She's really happy for us and wants to come to the wedding. I told her everything that's happened. She knows Matt, and was surprised that he's become so violent. Even when he was drinking, none of us ever saw that side of him before. Izzy's having big problems with Bruce though. She let him come over last night. She was going to tell him she didn't want to see him any more. He tried to sweet talk her at first. He told her if she'd just go to bed with him, she'd change her mind. She kept saying no. Then he got mad and threw her down on the bed. He held her down and tore off her clothes. When he let go of her to undo his pants, she grabbed her cell phone and hit him over the head with it. It didn't knock him out, but it surprised and stunned him."

Dwayne clapped his hands together. "Good for her, your friend's got a lot of spunk."

"Yes, but Izzy said that made him even angrier and more determined. He unzipped his pants and took down his shorts, but by then she was madder than he was, and had devised a strategy. She lay there quietly while he finished undressing and got on the bed. As soon as he was close enough, she let him have it with her knee to his groin. She said there was a moment of silence, then a gasp and a screech, and Bruce lay curled up on the bed clutching his privates. Izzy said he was out of commission long enough for her to put on her robe and get the poker from the fireplace. She came back into the bedroom waiving the poker in one hand, and her cell phone in the other. She told him he had two minutes to get out, or she'd call the police. He scrambled to get his clothes and left half dressed."

Dwayne shook his head. "Unbelievable! Is she going to call the police? I heard you trying to talk her into it."

"I hope so. She didn't think they'd arrest him since he didn't actually rape her. But he certainly attempted it, and who knows, he might have a record. What if he's a serial rapist? At least she'll be safe at my place. What a thing to happen. Dating is the pits, it's just too scary out there."

"That's for sure." Dwayne put his arms around Melanie and held her. "We're so lucky to have found each other. I love you Mel."

"I love you too." Melanie kissed him, then called Rhonda and explained the situation. Rhonda was appalled. Her husband had died four years ago. She'd stopped dating because of the bad experiences she'd had, but none were as horrifying as this. She said she'd watch for Izzy and keep an eye on things.

Chapter 23 – The Walters

The Walters' family arrived late in the afternoon. Craig called Dwayne from the car, and Dwayne told him how to open the gate. While they were driving up the road, Ida called the family together and suggested they stay in the house until the children were inside. "We should approach them one by one. Greeting them all together like we usually do might be too overwhelming." Everyone agreed, and they watched from the window as the rental car pulled up.

Craig got out and opened the door on the passenger side for Mr. Walters. He helped him out of the car, and handed him his cane. The two little girls got out of the back seat and tentatively looked around. Craig shook hands with Dwayne. "Hi, it's so nice of you to have us here."

"It's our pleasure. We're so glad you could all come." Dwayne walked over to Mr. Walters and put his hand out. "I'm sorry for your loss, Mr. Walters. I hope you will find some comfort here at the ranch."

"Thank you, and please call me Lawrence. Nancy couldn't come. She had to make dinner."

Julie ran over to Craig and grabbed his hand, whispering, "There he goes again."

Dwayne looked startled. He turned to Craig, who threw up his hands in a gesture that said "I don't know." Dwayne kneeled down by the little girl. "You must be Julie."

"Uh huh" Julie nodded.

Dwayne shook her hand. "We have something special to show you later. Tiger just had six kittens, and they need someone to play with."

Susan came over. "Hello. My name is Susan Walters. My grandmother's heart attacked her and she died. We all cried. Are the kittens real or just stuffed?"

"Hi Susan, I'm Dwayne, and I'm happy to meet you. I'm so sorry about your grandmother. I heard she was a wonderful person. The kittens are as real as can be. They're soft, and cuddly, and love to play. I'll show you where they are after dinner. Come in the house now, and meet the rest of the family." Dwayne ushered them inside, than he and Craig went to unload the car. When they were out of earshot he asked "What's with Mr. Walters?"

Craig shrugged. "You know, he's been getting more forgetful over the years, but since Nancy died, he can't remember anything except things from long ago. He either can't accept that she died, or doesn't remember it. He mixes the girls' names up, and sometimes calls me Matt. I'm at my wits end to know what to do. He can't take care of the children, and right now I'm in no position to take them full time either. Frankly, if you hadn't suggested coming here, I don't know what I would have done."

Dwayne frowned. "That's too bad. Maybe we can work out a plan while you're here."

Tom and Ida met the Walters' family at the door, with Melanie close behind. They introduced themselves, and Ida said, "Do come in, and a big welcome to you all. I was very sorry to hear about your grandmother. I know you must have loved her very much."

Julie spoke up. "We did. Grandma took care of us because our Mommy died, and Daddy drinks too much beer, and Grandpa is distabled. Now Craig takes care of us."

Melanie held her hand out to Susan. "And it looks like he's doing a wonderful job. I'm Melanie, Dwayne's fiancée."

"What's a feensay? Is it a good thing to be? Can I be one too?"

Melanie smiled. "I'll tell you what, tonight we'll talk and I'll tell you all about it. Right now we have lots to do. But first come inside and meet the others." She took the little girls by the hand and led them over to Jody. "Aunt Jody, meet Julie and Susan." Jody kneeled down and opened her arms. The two girls came to her and yielded to her hug, immediately trusting her.

"Hello. I am so glad to meet you. We've all looked forward to your visit. We fixed up a bedroom especially for you. There are lots of toys and things to do here." Jody stood up and turned to Lawrence. "I'm so sorry to hear about your wife. You're to be commended for taking such good care of these little girls. I hope your stay here will be pleasant."

"Thank you. I'm sure it will. Nancy will be along soon."

Everyone looked up with startled expressions on their faces.

"Grandpa keeps forgetting that Grandma died." Susan explained.

Hilda came in and introduced herself. "Hi, I'm Hilda. I've taken care of this family for many years, and I can tell you, they don't come any finer. Please let me know if you need anything. Hello," she said to the girls. "Let's see. Who's Julie and who's Susan?"

"I'm Susan and I'm six. Julie's four. She's just a baby."

Julie stamped her foot. "I am not a baby. I'm going to kindergarten next year."

"Of course you are." Hilda took the girls' hands and led them into the kitchen. Their grandfather followed. "This is Luz and Marcus. They're responsible for all the good cooking, and for these yummy cookies. Dinner's not ready yet. Would you like a cookie and some milk?"

"Yes," said Julie. "Chocolate chip please." Hilda showed them where to wash their hands, and sat them down at the kitchen table, then offered cookies and coffee to the others. Julie took a drink of her milk. "We got to fly right through a cloud, and the pilot came and talked to us. Look, the captain gave us wings, and they x-rayed our suitcases in case we brought anything dangerous. They took grandpa's razor. That was pretty silly."

Susan continued the story. "It was fun until that baby started crying. My heavens, what a racket it made." Susan looked at the ceiling and put her hands over her ears, mimicking her grandmother. Everyone laughed.

Tom downed a cookie. "If you're finished, come with us and we'll show you your rooms." They led them to the west end of the house, than realized Lawrence wasn't with them. Jody and Dwayne went to look for him. They found him in the library, gazing at the books with a smile of recognition on his face. Jody went to him and asked "Do you like our library?"

"Yes, reading is my favorite thing." Lawrence took down a book of poetry and opened it. He recited from memory:

"How I do love to go up in a swing, up in the air so blue.
Oh I do think it the pleasantest thing, ever a child can do.
Up in the air and over the wall, 'til I can see so wide.
Rivers and trees and cattle, and all over the countryside.
'Til I look down on the garden green, down on the roof so brown.
Then up in the air I go flying again, up in the air and down."

"Robert Lewis Stevenson, I think."

Jody whispered something to Dwayne and he nodded. "Lawrence, I think you'll be most comfortable in here. The bed's comfy, and there's a bathroom right next door. We'll bring your clothes in so you can get settled."

Lawrence looked at Jody. "Yes. Nancy will like this room too. She likes me to read to her in the evening."

Jody took his arm. "Dwayne, I'm going to stay with Lawrence for a while and show him where everything is."

Dwayne nodded agreement and went to get Lawrence's suitcase.

Tom and Ida led Julie and Susan to the room they'd fixed up for them. Julie saw the teddy bear on the bed and ran straight for it, then stopped. "May I touch him?"

"Of course," Ida said. "He told me earlier that he needs a hug."

Julie picked him up and hugged him tight. "Does he have a name?"

"No, and he needs one. You can choose a name for him."

Susan spotted the doll on the other bed. "Look, it's a grandma doll. I've never seen one like that before. She's got wings and a halo, like an angel. Does that mean her soul is in heaven like my grandmother?"

Melanie knelt down next to Susan. "It sounds like your grandma was already an angel when she was here on earth, so I wouldn't be surprised if God made her an angel in heaven right away. Would you like to hold her?"

"Yes." Susan took the doll and hugged it. She kept it with her the rest of the day, and slept with it when they were finally tucked under the covers.

Julie opened the toy box. "Oh boy, a tea set, and a Barbie doll. Look, she has a wedding dress and a bikini so she can go swimming. Here's a pony with a real saddle." Susan went to look, and the girls soon had most of the toys laid out on the floor, trying to decide what to play with first.

The dinner bell rang, and the family ushered their new guests into the dining room. Luz and Marcus brought out roast chickens they'd basted until the skins were brown and crispy. They passed around bowls of mashed potatoes and gravy. There was a salad made of greens and cherry tomatoes picked fresh from the garden. The rolls were warm from the oven, and smelled delicious.

Tom folded his hands. "I'd like to thank the Lord for giving us the privilege of meeting all these wonderful folks. I know he's taking good care of Nancy Walters up there, and I thank him for that too. Now, let's eat." The others nodded amen, and attacked the food.

After dinner, Craig put jackets on Julie and Susan, and they all went up to the barn. The kittens were full of energy. Tiger sat in a corner and watched their goings on. The kittens wrestled and batted each other's tails. Every once in a while, one bounced off Tiger, but she kept them at a distance. The orange kitten sat very still, watching Tiger's tail batting back and forth. Suddenly she leaped in the air and landed smack on her tail. Tiger let out a meow and shook her off. Restoring her dignity, Tiger walked over to Melanie with her tail in the air and jumped into her lap.

The girls went from one kitten to the other, picking each one up and hugging it, then putting it down to pick up another. Susan found a long piece of hay and trailed it this way and that in front of the kittens. The orange one ran after it, trying to grab it with her paw. "This one should be called Orange Popsicle. She's so cute. Look how long her whiskers are."

Dwayne laughed. "Cats use their whiskers to measure things, so they grow as wide as their bodies. We've been trying to figure out which one to keep, but I think you've decided for us. Orange Popsicle is the perfect name. We can call her Pops for short. They'll stay in the barn a couple more weeks until they're completely weaned. Then Pops will come to live with us in the ranch house. The others are promised to other families."

They stayed and played with the kittens until Julie starting yawning. When they got back to the house, they found that Craig had unpacked the girls' clothes, and laid their pajamas on the beds. He helped them wash up, and made sure they brushed their teeth. Craig brought Lawrence in to hear their prayers and tuck them under the quilts. "Julie, it's your turn to tell the story."

"Okay, but I'm pretty sleepy." She told about the plane ride, and the pilot, and the clouds outside the windows that looked like cotton candy. "Then we came to the ranch, and played with the kittens, and named one Orange Popsicle," she said, yawning between sentences. "I named the Teddy bear Teddio. Can he sleep with me?" Craig handed her the bear and she wrapped her arms around it. "Goodnight." She said, and blew a kiss.

Susan was sitting up in bed, also yawning. She had propped the doll's head on the pillow next to her, and tucked the covers around it. "This is a nice place. Can we go swimming tomorrow?"

"We'll see what the weather's like. Goodnight now." Craig tucked her in and went to join the others.

Dwayne showed Craig the second bedroom. "We had intended to put Lawrence in here, but it's obvious he'll feel more at home in the library. This used to be my digs. I think you'll find it comfortable."

Craig scratched his head. "It's really nice, but you know, I still smoke. It's the only bad habit I haven't been able to kick. I've been sober for two years, and have a steady girl. Watching Matt made me realize how destructive drinking was. Besides, if I was going to get him to quit, I had to do it first. Anyway, I brought my sleeping bag. Is there a place out in the woods where I could sleep under the stars?"

"Actually there is, if you don't mind the coyotes." Dwayne told the story, and Craig laughed as he pictured the men staggering around marking everything in sight. "I don't think the coyotes will be back. Come on back to the house about seven. Luz serves a great a breakfast. Would you like to ride out with Melanie and me tomorrow? We do a run around the ranch every morning to check on things. We can take the girls too."

"That would be great. I used to ride a lot, and I miss it." Craig pulled out his checkbook. "I want to pay for our room and board, just as if we were guests. What should I write the check for?"

Dwayne put his hand up. It's so nice of you to offer, but really, there's no need. We're doing this because we feel a kinship with you, and my family is getting far more from this experience than money could ever buy. Just having you all here, and being able to help the children heal is a treasure. Thank you for your offer though."

Craig sighed. "That is so great of you. Thanks, and please thank the rest of the family for me."

"Okay then, we'll see you in the morning."

Dwayne went to see how Lawrence was faring. He was taking his clothes out of the drawer, folding them neatly, and putting them back into the suitcase. Dwayne found his pajamas and handed them to him. "Here, its time for bed now. Let's put these shirts back in the drawer. Would you like some help getting your pajamas on?"

Lawrence took the pajamas. "No, I can do it. I think I'll go to bed early. I'm really tired, and Nancy's coming tomorrow." Dwayne put the empty suitcases on the top closet shelf. He waited to make sure Lawrence got his pajamas on and got into bed, then went to turn off the light. Lawrence waived his hand. "Leave the light on please. Nancy doesn't like the dark."

"Okay, goodnight."

Dwayne joined the family. They were talking about Mr. Walters. Melanie was describing some of the elderly patients at the hospital who were like him. "They can't remember where they are, or what just happened, but they can remember very complex things that happened long ago. Lawrence may have dementia, or possibly early Alzheimer's. Either condition could have been exacerbated by his wife's death. He may improve in a couple of days when the shock wears off."

Dwayne nodded. "He's in bed now. He was putting his things back in the suitcase. He does take suggestions, though, and is able to dress himself. He's still thinking Nancy is coming here tomorrow. What a shame, and just when the kids need him the most."

Jody stood up. "I don't think we should leave the girls alone in the west wing. They may need something during the night. I'm going to move some of my things into Dwayne's bedroom, and sleep there while they're with us. I'll be able to hear them from there."

Dwayne and Melanie lay awake talking for a long time. "The grandmother did a good job bringing up those children. Susan is smart, and so outspoken, and Julie is adorable. They seem aware of their circumstances. It appears that they've accepted their father and grandfather for who they are."

Dwayne nodded. "They're great kids all right. I had a talk with Craig. He said he stopped drinking two years ago, and kicked all his other bad habits. Too bad he can't stop smoking. The grandfather is an interesting person. He's obviously well educated. Do you really think his memory might improve?"

"If it's just shock and dementia, it's very possible. It's the nature of that disease to come and go. When a senile person is having a good day, he can converse with you like a normal person. Then, a day or two later, he may not remember who you are."

Dwayne stood up and stretched. "Hey Mel, will you still love me when we're old and gray and I call you Gracie?" He gave her a friendly pat and they fell down together on the bed, laughing and wrestling.

"Dwayne, you're such a smart ass. And your lips taste so sweet. I love you, but I'm too tired to do anything about it now, so prepare for an attack in the morning. Right now I'm already a s l e e p." She let her voice trail off, and Dwayne cuddled up against her.

True to her promise, Melanie woke up early. She looked at Dwayne, and an urgent longing for him began to stir deep within her. She wanted to touch him, but didn't want to wake him. She watched him sleep for a while, than went into the bathroom. Melanie looked in the mirror, thinking out loud. "I really love that man. It's such a good feeling, nothing like what I felt with Matt." She looked through her case and found a bottle of almond massage oil. She brought it back to bed, and slipped out of her gown. Dwayne was sleeping on his side. She crept under the covers and edged over to him. She put some oil on her hands, rubbing them together to warm them. Then, ever so softly, she spread the oil on his back.

Dwayne stirred. "Mmm, that feels good. Do that some more." Melanie added more oil to her hand, and reached around to stroke it onto his chest. Dwayne wriggled, "Oh Mel, you're making me crazy!" Melanie slid her hand down over his belly and inched her way under his pajamas. She stroked him softly all over, then found what she was looking for.

Dwayne groaned and turned to her. He pushed his pajamas out of the way. "Can I have some of that?" Melanie put some oil in his hand, and he let it drip onto her breasts. He stroked her softly, watching the look of ecstasy on her face. He moved his hand down to the place he knew she liked best. He caressed her gently until she arched her back and cried out. Dwayne held her and kissed her until her passion rose again. They joined together and moved slowly at first, then with more intensity, until their hunger for each other was again satisfied. They held each other close, and Melanie whispered in Dwayne's ear, "I love you so much. And you are so delicious. I can't seem to get enough of you. I was watching you sleep, and my imagination ran wild."

Dwayne grinned. "I love you too, and I love your imagination." He suddenly broke away. "Hey, do all your clients get this kind of treatment?" He folded his hands across his chest and made a face.

Melanie laughed. "Absolutely not, my clients only get a professional massage. The hanky panky is just for you. Come on, let's go shower. We can soap each other up and wash off the oil." A new stirring started in Dwayne's loins, and he felt like a teen again. They showered and teased and played together, then dried off and got dressed.

It was still early when Melanie and Dwayne came through to the main house. It seemed at first that only the kitchen staff were up. Then they saw Jody sitting on the sofa. Julie was sitting on her lap, with Susan close by. Jody was reading one of the books they'd brought from the hospital. Melanie and Dwayne stopped to listen. "...so your memories of your grandmother will always be with you."

There was a moment of quiet, than Julie said. "Grandma used to take Susan to school in the morning. After school we'd pick her up and go to ballet class. We have shiny pink ballet slippers. We can't go up on our toes yet. You have to be older to do that. Grandma was a good cook. She made French toast for breakfast."

Susan interrupted. "I like ballet dancing. When I grow up, I'm going to join a dance company in New York, but first I want to be a cheerleader. When we watched them on TV, Grandma always said no way, it's too dangerous. I told her not to worry because I'll always be the one on the bottom holding the others up. I'm not going to stand on someone's shoulders with them jumping around cheering."

"I should say not." Jody said. "Cheerleaders are very different nowadays. When I was in school, they **all** stayed on the ground."

"Bor—ing." Susan said, emphasizing the bor. "It's more exciting the way they do it now, as long as I get to be on the bottom."

Dwayne and Melanie came into the room. "Good morning. Sounds like you two have a busy life. Did you ever ride a horse?"

Susan nodded. "Craig took us for a pony ride once, but we just walked around in a circle. I like horses. Do you have any here?"

"You bet. We have some beauties, and they don't like going in circles either. How would you like to go riding with us after chapel?

We'll ride around the ranch and show you all the things you can do here. Julie, you can ride with Craig. Susan, you can ride with me on Jenny."

Julie scrambled off Jody's lap and jumped up and down. "Oh boy. We're going on a real horseback ride. Come on, let's go." She ran for the door.

Susan put her hands on her hips. "Silly, you can't go in your jammies. We have to get dressed first."

Jody laughed. "Right you are. Let's get some clothes on. We'll have breakfast and go to chapel, than you can go riding." Jody found some jeans and shirts in their closet. She helped them wash up, and brushed their hair. Tennis shoes and baseball caps completed their outfits.

Julie went to her grandfather's room and knocked on the door. Grampa, are you up? We're going horseback riding. Do you want to come?"

"Are you now? Well good for you. I think I'll pass on the riding though." Lawrence was already dressed. He was sitting in a rocking chair, reading a book of poetry. Julie grabbed his hand and led him into the dining room. Luz had fixed ham and scrambled eggs, and there was blackberry jam to spread on the hot biscuits.

Craig joined them, also dressed for riding in boots and a western shirt. "No sign of a coyote last night." Craig held his nose. "It's a little stinky in the woods though. You guys did a good job. I think you chased off every critter for miles around." Everyone laughed.

The girls chattered away as they finished eating. "Okay, let's go to chapel so we can go riding." Julie jumped up and down, than stopped. "Hey, what's chapel?" she asked breathlessly.

"It's a church we have on the ranch, right at the top of the hill. We always have a short meeting there on Sunday. Tom turned to Lawrence. If it's okay with you, we'd like to dedicate today's service to your wife."

"That would be very nice, Nancy will like that. She'll be here soon."

Tom started the service with a short prayer, than organized everyone into a circle. "Now take hands. I'll start." He paused for a moment and closed his eyes. "I am grateful for my faith that Nancy Walters is in heaven, being taken care of by the Lord."

They went around the circle and each person took their turn. It was a beautiful ceremony. Even the children's statements were thoughtful and heartwarming.

It was Lawrence's turn last. He was quiet for a long time. Then he said, "Nancy was always there to help us. She was very generous with her love, and with her time. I miss her very much." His voice cracked and he stopped for a moment, than said, "I'm very grateful for these wonderful folks who've taken us in, and are going out of their way to help us through these trying times. Thanks to all of you, and thank you God." Tears were in everyone's eyes as he finished talking. They let go of each others' hands and hugged all around.

Dwayne and Melanie led Susan and Julie to the stables, and the others went back to the house. The children oohed and aahed when they saw the horses. Julie jumped up and down. "That one's really big. Look at him! He's looking at me. Can I ride him?"

"He's a good horse, but we're going to ride my favorite, Jenny." Melanie was already leading Danny out of the stall. Lance came over to help. This is Lance. He knows horses better than anybody, and he can answer any questions you may have. We need another gentle one for Craig and Susan. Which one do you recommend?"

Lance led them over to a brown and white Pinto. "Mickey's really good with kids, what do you think?"

"Of course," Dwayne said, "Tommy used to ride Mickey. Tommy was our foster child. He loved horses. Okay, let's saddle them up."

Julie and Susan watched every step as the horses were saddled, asking questions about everything. Julie tried to lift the saddle onto the Pinto. Lance laughed. "Better let me do that. It's pretty heavy."

At last all was ready. Dwayne mounted Jenny, and Craig got on Mickey. Lance lifted Julie onto the saddle, and Craig put his arm around her waist. Then he boosted Susan onto Jenny in front of Dwayne. Julie patted Mickey's mane shouting, "Okay, giddyup Mickey Mouse." Susan giggled.

Dwayne waited while Lance adjusted Melanie's stirrups. "Okay, are we ready? Let's go then." They started off slowly, walking the horses down the hill toward the swimming pool. "Can we go in the pool later?" Susan asked. "I can swim, but Julie has to stay in the baby pool."

"I do not. I learned really good last summer. Remember?"

Craig held up his hand. "Now don't quarrel girls. Maybe we can go for a swim later if it warms up a little."

They circled the pool and rode over to the garden. Susan pointed at the vines that had crept through the fence. "Look at those big pumpkins." They're way bigger than me! Can we pick some?"

"They're not ready yet, and they're much too big to carry back. We'll pick them for Halloween and bring them to the house in the truck."

Craig looked at the huge garden. "Hey, this is great. You grow everything here. Boy, I wish we had something like this in New York. Their produce is the pits, and we only get half-decent stuff during the summer."

Melanie stopped in front of the herb garden that was planted in pots along the back side of the fence. "That's the most beautiful spider I've ever seen." She pointed to a large black and yellow-orange spider with what looked like long black fingernails on the ends of its legs. Its huge web was perfectly symmetrical.

"That's a female Argiope, the orb spider I told you about." Dwayne pointed to the middle of the web. "See the zigzag purple thread? She has a special gland that spins that out after the web is done. It attracts insects and moths. If too many insects get tangled in the web at the same time, she'll run over and stab them. She injects something in them to paralyze them. Then she wraps each of them up like little cocoons until she's ready for lunch."

"Eeeuw." Julie screwed up her face. "Would she stab me if I fell in the web?"

"She probably wouldn't mix with anything as big as you, but be careful, it takes all night to repair the web. See how big her abdomen is. She's carrying a brood of eggs. A male is hiding in the rosemary, waiting to fertilize them. She'll spin an incredible nest to hold the eggs until they hatch next spring. The nest looks like a thimble with a cover on it. It's light, but very strong and well insulated."

They watched the spider for a while, than headed towards Anabelle's pen. Tom hadn't found anyone to take George yet. There he was, nursing away, while Gracie looked on from a distance. Dwayne dismounted, helped Susan down from Jenny, and ducked under the fence. "You all stay put. The bull's still little, but he's already mighty aggressive." He threw the rope around George, and led him away from

Anabelle so Gracie could nurse. Gracie had gained some weight, with the diligent help of the ranch hands, and she looked like a miniature of Anabelle. When Gracie had had her fill, Dwayne ducked back under the fence and lifted Susan back onto Jenny, then swung on behind her. The last stop was the barn, and they dismounted to play with the kittens.

Part VI

Chapter 24 – Bruce

Izzy keyed in a new chapter. She read what she'd written and scowled. She moved the cursor to "edit," and slid it down to "select all." She hit the backspace key, and watched her morning's efforts disappear from the screen. "What a wasted day," she said out loud. "I'll try again tomorrow. What I really need is a chocolate fix, and to get out of this apartment for a while. I think I'll run over to Trader Joe's and get some of those chocolate-covered cranberries. Maybe that'll inspire me to do something."

Izzy shut down the computer, grabbed her purse and keys, and locked the apartment. She knocked on her neighbor's door, and Rhonda popped her head out. "I'm going stir crazy in there, and I can't write anything to save my soul. I'm going to Trader Joe's to get something decadent. Want to come?"

"I'd love to, but I'm expecting a call from my daughter. Her baby's due any time, and I want to be able to shoot over to the hospital as soon as she calls. Can you get me something though? I love their vanilla yogurt."

The parking lot was full, but Izzy saw someone pulling out of a space in front of the center, and she eased into it. She took her time walking around the store, reading labels, and tossing things into the cart. When she got to the check stand, she laughed when she saw that her chocolate craving yielded two paper bags full of delectables. She stowed them in the trunk, taking the cranberries with her to nibble in the car.

She parked in front of the apartment building, and got the grocery bags. She set them down in front of Rhonda's door and rang the doorbell. "Rhonda, its Izzy. Here's your yogurt." No answer. She picked up the bags, unlocked Melanie's apartment, and brought them into the kitchen. She unloaded everything onto the counter, and was putting the yogurt in the refrigerator when she heard steps behind her. "Hi Rhonda here's your yo …" Izzy turned, than stopped dead. Bruce was standing there. He had a long kitchen knife in one hand, and a ball of twine in the other.

"Hey Izzy. I've been trying to find you. You should have told me you moved. I knew you'd eventually go to Trader's, so I've been waiting there for you every afternoon. It wasn't very nice of you not to tell me your new address."

Izzy drew herself up and walked confidently toward Bruce. "You get out of here or I'm going to call the police."

"Not so fast." Bruce came toward her waving the knife. "I brought some stuff to help convince you to marry me, and I don't want to get interrupted like last time."

Izzy tried to think. Was he bluffing? No way. He'd waited for her, and followed her here, and now he was coming toward her with a knife. She looked around for something—anything to defend herself with. She picked up the teapot and threw it at Bruce. He dodged and moved closer to her, backing her up against the counter. He waived the knife in front of her face, then rested the point on her neck. Izzy tried to knock it away, but the sharp knife grazed her. Blood started dripping down her arm and onto the floor.

Bruce frowned. "Now you be nice and I won't hurt you. You don't want to be all cut up for the wedding do you? Now you just back up into the bedroom, and I'll show you what our honeymoon's going to be like."

"You're crazy. You don't think I'd marry you, or even touch you after this?"

"It'll be real good Izzy. You'll see. You won't be able to resist me," he said sweetly. Then his voice changed. "Besides, you owe me from last time. Now hurry up so I won't have to hurt you." Keeping the knife pressed against her throat, Bruce backed Izzy into the bedroom, and pushed her roughly onto the bed. He held the knife with one hand, and with the other, tied her left wrist to the headboard. She tried to grab the knife with the other hand, but Bruce was strong. He soon had both her hands tied securely to the bed. He took hold of her shirt at the neckline and slit it down the front, then did the same with her bra.

Izzy thrashed around, trying to get loose. She tried to kick him, but he dodged out of reach.

"Oh no you don't. You know you really hurt me last time. I have a better way to do it now. Watch."

Bruce wrapped a length of twine around Izzy's right ankle and tied it to the bedpost. She kicked at him with her left foot, but he moved out of reach. He grabbed her left foot and firmly tied it too, leaving her immobile and completely vulnerable. Izzy screamed, than remembered that Rhonda wasn't home. The reality of what was going to happen washed over her. She struggled to free herself, but the twine dug into her wrists and ankles.

Bruce unzipped her jeans. He tried to pull them down, along with her panties, but her legs were spread apart. He swore, than cut them off her, cutting her legs in several places. Izzy screamed again. Bruce put the knife point on her cheek and drew it across to her mouth, drawing a thin line of blood. "Now you keep quiet. I just want a little kiss first." Bruce threw the knife on the floor, undressed, and got on top of her. He put his mouth on hers and lowered his body. Izzy could feel him trying to probe his way in. She opened her mouth and bit his lip as hard as she could. Bruce jumped away, and felt blood dripping down his chin. He slapped Izzy hard across the face. "You little bitch. You're going to get it now." He lowered himself onto her again. Just then, the doorbell rang. Bruce froze, and Izzy could feel him shrink in fear. In spite of the terror she felt, she still had the presence to be tickled by his ineptitude when under fire. She promised herself to add this to her next novel.

She called out as loud as she could. "Help! Help me, I'm being raped!"

Bruce recovered somewhat, and put his hand over her mouth whispering menacingly. "Shut up." He saw the knife on the floor, and let go of her to reach for it.

Izzy screamed again, shouting "Help! Please help me!"

Bruce put the knife to her throat, and put his hand roughly back over her mouth. "One more word from you and you're finished."

Izzy hoped whoever was at the door had heard her, but it was quiet, and she figured they were already long gone. A minute passed. Then she heard a key turn in the lock. Suddenly someone burst into the bedroom. "Okay, you—get off her. Melanie, are you all right?"

Izzy looked up in surprise. It was Matt Walters, Melanie's ex-boyfriend. He was holding a pistol aimed right at them! Melanie had told her Matt had stolen a gun from a cabin at the ranch, and had broken into her apartment, conked her on the head, and left her with a broken leg. She didn't know who to be more afraid of, Bruce with his knife trying to rape her, or Matt waiving a gun at them. "Matt, it's Izzy. Melanie's not here. What are you doing here? Please help me. This guy is trying to rape me, and he's got a knife."

Matt saw the blood on Izzy's face and arm. He grabbed Bruce and pulled him off her, then whacked him hard on the head with the gun. The knife dropped to the floor and Bruce slumped over. Matt picked him up, dragged him over to a wooden rocking chair, and sat him down. He took the ball of twine, cut some pieces with the knife, and tied Bruce's arms to the chair. He strung a length around his neck and tied it to the back of the rocker. Seeing that Izzy was naked, he threw a corner of the bedspread over her. He cut the ropes on her wrists and ankles. "Are you all right? Is Melanie all right? Where is she?" Matt looked around, expecting to see Melanie tied up in a corner.

"She's not here. I've been using her apartment because this jerk has been stalking me. Matt, thank goodness you're here, but ..." Izzy paused, then asked, "How did you know I was being—you thought Mel was here. Why do you have a gun with you?" A shiver a fear ran down Izzy's back as she waited for the answers.

"It's a long story. Don't worry, I'm not drunk, and I'm not dangerous. I wasn't coming after Melanie, and I'm certainly not going to hurt you. I know this looks crazy, but believe me, I can explain everything. I came to bring Melanie's things back and tell her I was sorry. The gun was in the bag with her stuff. When I heard you yell for help, I grabbed it and let myself in. I still have the key. Why don't you get dressed. I'll go make some coffee, than fill you in on the rest of the details." Izzy nodded.

Matt went into the kitchen. Everything was as he remembered, and he found the coffee and filters where he and Melanie had always kept them. A vision of the last time he'd been at the apartment flashed over him, and he tucked the memory away to deal with later.

Izzy looked at Bruce. He was still out cold. She grabbed some jeans and a shirt from the closet and got dressed, then went to find Matt.

"I'm going to call the police," she said tentatively, not knowing what his reaction would be. She went for the phone.

Matt held up his hand. "Wait, I already called them. They should be here in a few minutes."

She breathed a sigh of relief. If Matt had called the police, she guessed he was okay. Izzy sat down and thought about the situation, then dissolved into giggles. She laughed until tears ran down her cheeks. Matt soon realized the tears were for real. He went to her and held her until she'd cried herself out. Izzy grabbed a tissue. She explained that only Bruce's shrinking organ when he'd heard the doorbell had kept her from going completely to pieces when he was on top of her. "It was a good thing you were here though. That was way too close for comfort."

Matt poured coffee for both of them. "Do you know that guy, or did he just break in?"

Izzy made a face. "I dated him for while. He said he was an attorney. I was attracted to him because he was tall and good looking. He seemed to be intelligent, but he turned out to be a maniac. His mother told me he's been disbarred. He's been stalking me, and this is the second time he's tried to rape me. If you hadn't shown up, I'm afraid he would have succeeded. He said if I would sleep with him, I'd want to marry him because he was so irresistible. The horror of it overcame Izzy and her stomach lurched. She ran to the bathroom and gave up the cranberries.

The doorbell rang. Matt let two police officers in, both with guns in their hands. One of them leveled her gun at Matt. "Okay, hands over your head."

"Wait, not me!" Matt waived his hands over his head and tried to explain, but they wouldn't listen. The other officer frisked him, looking for the knife.

Izzy came into the room. "No, no. You've got the wrong guy. It's Bruce who tried to rape me. He's in the other room."

"Sorry," they said, and let go of Matt. "I'm Officer Cruz, and this is Officer Draper. We heard there's been some trouble here." They followed Matt and Izzy into the bedroom.

Bruce was just coming to. He looked in disbelief at the policemen. He tried to get up, but found he was securely tied to the chair. He struggled to clear his head. "I'm so glad you're here officers. This man broke into the house and threatened me with a gun. He hit me over the head, and tied me to this chair. I'm an attorney, and I'm going to see that he's put away for B&E and assault and battery. Now untie me, please."

Officer Draper untied the twine that was wound around Bruce's neck. "Now wait a minute," she said. "Someone reported a rape from here. Who made that call?"

Matt stepped up. "I did. When I rang the doorbell, I heard Izzy yelling for help. I used to live here, and still had the key. I came in and saw this jerk holding a knife to her throat. There it is." Matt reached for the knife on the floor.

Cruz stopped him. "Wait, don't touch that. What made you think he'd raped her?"

Matt pointed to the twine still clinging to the bedposts. "He'd tied Izzy to the bed. He'd cut her clothes off and was on top of her naked."

"Is that his gun you hit him with?"

Matt put his head down. "No sir, it isn't. The gun belongs to a friend of mine. I was just returning it. It's a long story."

Izzy took over and told what happened from the beginning. "What Matt is saying is true, and this rotten no good—has been stalking me for a week. And he's not a lawyer any more. He's been disbarred. This is the second time he's tried to rape me. I filed a police report the first time, but he twisted everything. The police said since I'd dated him before, and had invited him to come over, they couldn't arrest him. That's why I'm staying at my friend's apartment. Then this afternoon, he waited for me at Trader Joe's and followed me here."

Cruz looked at Bruce. "Is this true?" Bruce was silent. She wrote something on her report, than looked at Izzy. "Ma'am, did this man achieve penetration today?"

Izzy shook her head. "No he didn't, although he tried. But if Matt hadn't rung the doorbell when he did, the story might have been different. Bruce hit me on the face, and cut me with the knife." Izzy showed the officer the cuts on her cheek, neck and arm. "My legs too. I was afraid he was going to kill me."

"Then I assume you want to press charges. Would you be willing to come down to the station and file a report on what happened here today?"

"Absolutely." Izzy said. Matt nodded agreement.

"Okay, we're going to get him dressed and read him his rights, then take him in on your say so. You two follow us back to headquarters."

"Okay. Thanks Officers."

The phone rang. It was Rhonda reporting that her daughter had just given birth to a nine pound baby boy. Izzy congratulated her. "I have your yogurt. I'll give it to you when you get home, along with a most unbelievable story."

"So you're writing again. Good," Rhonda said, thinking Izzy meant a chapter in her book.

"Nope, this one's the real thing. I'll tell you all about it when I see you. Tell your daughter congrats, and kiss that baby for me."

Izzy and Matt followed the police car to the station, and the officers took down their statements. Officer Draper took Izzy into a private room. They questioned her again about the extent of the attack. They took photos of the cuts, and the red welt on her face where Bruce had slapped her.

Officer Cruz found the first report Izzy had made. "There'll be a hearing in a couple of days. I don't know if bail will be granted. Usually in cases like this, the judge won't allow it. If he does, and if Bruce can come up with the money, he'll be out on the streets again, so keep your doors locked. Here's a victim's card. It's got my number on it. It gives some tips to help you stay safe until the trial. Call me if you have any more trouble."

Izzy was quiet as they drove back to Melanie's apartment. "Will you come in Matt? I could sure use some of that coffee now."

"Me too" said Matt, "and some of those cookies I saw on the counter."

Izzy poured coffee and opened the package of cookies. "You know, I can't believe they might let that bastard off on bail. I swear if they let him go, and he tries to get into this house, I'll kill him."

Matt shook his head. "I know how you feel, but remember, unless he puts his hands on you first, and it's a clear case of self defense, you're liable to end up in jail instead of him. Having been an attorney, he'll have a whole battery of tricks to make it look like you attacked him first. It could end up your word against his."

Izzy banged her fist on the table. "Damn, our system is really screwed up. They're busy protecting the rights of the perpetrators, when the victims are the ones who need protecting."

Matt nodded. "It's a mess all right."

Izzy sipped her coffee. In spite of the stress of the day, curiosity overcame her. "So tell me about you, Matt. I want to hear more about how you happened to be here just at the right moment. And I have some things to tell you too."

Chapter 25 – Matt

Matt sat down across from Izzy. "Some of what I'm going to tell you I haven't told Melanie. I don't know why I kept my past a secret from her, but I know that it was a big mistake." Matt told Izzy about his marriage and how his in-laws and wife died in the car crash. "I couldn't hold it together after that. I left the kids with a babysitter for long periods of time, and started drinking heavily. I lost my job. I did some day trading, and lost money in the stock market. Mom and Dad took the kids. I didn't fight them. I knew I couldn't take care of them in the state I was in. It took about a year before I pulled myself together and started working again. Then I met Melanie."

"So, you had stopped drinking when you met Mel?"

"Yes. Melanie and I were really happy. We even talked about getting married."

"You were talking marriage, but you didn't tell her about your children?"

"I know it sounds crazy. My thinking was all screwed up. I thought if she knew I had two little girls, and had left them with my parents, it would be all over between us. I'd planned to tell her when we actually got engaged. Things went well until a friend of hers got married. At the wedding, I drank a champagne toast to the bride and groom, and it set me off again. Melanie had to drive me home that night. I was so soused, I could hardly stand up. That was the end of our good relationship. Once I'd taken that drink, I just couldn't stop. The alcohol took over my life again, or rather, I let it take over. Even Melanie's threats of breaking up didn't bring me to my senses. She finally said I'd have to quit drinking or move out. She found an AA group nearby. I went to a meeting and looked in, but decided I could quit on my own.

I managed to stay sober for a couple of months, and told Melanie I was going to the meetings. Our last night together was a disaster. Melanie had planned a dinner celebrating our anniversary and my sobriety. I went out drinking with my buddies and came home soused and sick. She locked me out of the bedroom, and the next morning, asked me to leave."

"I went to New York and visited my family. I stayed with a friend for a while. He was a drinker too, but Craig could hold his liquor, and he knew when to stop. He told me I was an alcoholic, but I didn't believe him. It didn't make sense that he could take a drink or two and stop, but if I took just one, it would set off a ten-day binge. I did some terrible things. I was angry all the time. I took drugs, and hit some people. Craig bailed me out of jail a couple of times. I stopped seeing my kids and parents because I was so ashamed of what I'd become."

Izzy nodded sympathetically. "You were addicted, Matt. You couldn't help it. You seem fine today. How did you kick it?"

"I ran out of money and couldn't buy drugs, but I kept drinking. I called Melanie and made a date to see her. I lied and told her I was sober. Then I thought about keeping it together when I was with her, and I knew I couldn't do it. I called an old friend, and asked him to meet her for me, and tell her I didn't want to see her after all. I got to the point where I needed a fix really bad. I remembered some of the pushers I'd dealt with were willing to give credit for a while, but I didn't have their names or numbers. I'd written them down in an old address book I'd left at Melanie's. I rang the doorbell, but she wasn't home. I watched the apartment building, but she never showed up. I figured she'd gone with you to the beach. I still had the key to her apartment. When I saw her things, in my mind I transferred the blame for everything on Melanie. I was so angry. I tore up her apartment looking for the address book. I finally found it, and tore out the pages with the contacts' names. I took the Lladros and crystal cats I'd given her as gifts, and some other stuff I thought I might be able to pawn. But I couldn't sell anything. I never even took them out of the box."

"I sold some stock, and that kept me going for a while. Then I decided to visit an old friend who lives on a ranch up north. When I got there, I wasn't sure what kind of reception I was going to get, and I wasn't thinking clearly. Instead of going to the main house, I snuck around the back. When I got to the cabins, I saw Dwayne and Melanie walking up the path toward cabin nine, the one I used to stay in when I visited. They were talking and laughing. Melanie was carrying a pillow. They were teasing each other about who was going to use it. It was obvious they were together. I was crazy with jealousy. Later that night, when I looked in the window, I saw them in bed together."

"I slept in the woods. The next morning, Dwayne came around the back of the cabin. I watched from behind a tree. He seemed to be looking for something. I figured it was me. When they left, I tore the screen off the kitchen window and went in. I looked around the place, and looked under the bed. I have no idea what I was looking for. Then I opened some dresser drawers and saw the gun, and I took it. I went back into the woods and watched for a while. Melanie came back later that morning. She went into the cabin. She must have panicked when she saw the torn screen because she got out of there fast. A few minutes later, I saw a sheriff's car drive up to the main house. I got scared and took off. You know Izzy, I was completely nuts. I don't know anything about guns. I don't even know how to load a gun, let alone shoot it. It's a good thing I didn't have to shoot Bruce, because the pistol wasn't loaded."

Izzy laughed. "Thank God you had it with you though. It scared Bruce, and the blow knocked him cold. But Matt, what made you decide to come to the apartment today? Did you think Melanie would be here?"

"Yes I did. Breaking into my friend's cabin was like hitting bottom for me. I realized what a mess I'd made of my life. I'd lost my kids and my girlfriend. My parents were disgusted with me. I was flat broke, and couldn't afford to buy the booze my body was crying out for. Everyone kept telling me to go to AA, and something told me this was the time. When I walked into the meeting, I was greeted warmly. They gave me a cup of coffee and found me a seat. I was amazed at the people there. I thought I'd find a bunch of weirdos and neer-do-wells, but they were just ordinary people like you and me. A man introduced himself and said he was an alcoholic. Everyone responded, just like you see on TV. He told his story about his addiction, and losing his home and job, and how he'd hurt his family. Many parts of his story were similar to mine. I wasn't expecting that. He ended by saying he'd been sober for eight months, and everyone clapped. At the end, we got in a circle and said the serenity prayer. I've heard it many times, but it never meant anything to me until that day."

Izzy reached over and put her hand on Matt's arm. "Thank God you found that place. How long ago was that?"

"A couple of months. I haven't touched a drop since that meeting. It was tough at first. I was really sick, but my sponsor got me into a halfway house. We had AA meetings every night, and everyone supported each other. There were some rules. The first month you weren't allowed to leave the premises. The second month you could leave during the day to go to work, but had to be back at night. This month I'm free to come and go, and next month I'll be on my own. I plan to find a good job, and get a house or condo somewhere. I'd been working on the twelve steps, and got to the one about making amends to the people you've hurt. Melanie was high on my list, and I put the things I'd taken from her in the car. At the last minute, I went back and got the gun. When I rang the doorbell, I heard you scream. I thought it was Melanie." Matt took a deep breath. "Funny the strange turns life takes!"

Izzy nodded, dreading the things she was going to have to tell Matt. She looked at the clock. "It's after six and I've eaten nothing but junk food all day. Would you like to get a bite to eat somewhere?"

"That sounds good. I have to call the halfway house first." Can I use your phone?"

Izzy stood up. "Sure. I'm going to freshen up." She went in the bathroom and made a face at herself in the mirror. Her hair was going every which way, and she'd rubbed off her eye makeup. She put her face up close to the mirror to see the cuts on her neck and face, and the bruise where Bruce slapped her. She wondered if they would leave a scar. The cuts on her legs stung, and the one on her arm was red and swollen. She tried to think when she'd last had a tetanus shot, then her face blanched. My God, what if Bruce is HIV positive! She tried to remember whether he'd touched her wounds. No, she was certain that only the knife made contact, and his penis just barely touched her when the doorbell rang and scared it into a shrivel. She sighed in relief, but vowed to get a blood test just in case.

Izzy poured alcohol on a tissue and dabbed at the dried blood on the cuts. She traded her shirt for a long-sleeved white sweater. She put on some earrings, patched up her face, and brushed her hair. She tried to think how she could break the news to Matt about his mother dying, and Dwayne and Melanie's engagement. She concluded there was no easy way. She'd just have to tell him. She sighed and said to the mirror. "What a day this is, worse than any plot I could dream up for a novel." She grabbed a jacket.

Matt opened the car door for Izzy. "Is that Chinese place still around, the one on 9th?"

"It is, and they're still the best." They drove to Ming Lee's and were seated in a corner. They ordered egg rolls, mu shu chicken, asparagus beef, and fried rice. They spooned the stir-fry and plum sauce onto the thin pancakes, folded them into squares, and tried to keep the delicious juices from escaping as they ate. Izzy read the message from her fortune cookie out loud. "You will meet your soul mate soon. Hah!" she said, ripping the fortune into bits. "Soul mate! There's no such thing, men have no souls." She looked at Matt. "Present company excluded, of course." Matt smiled. "So what will you do next?" she asked, still avoiding the things she would eventually have to tell him.

"Well, after Melanie gets back, I'll tell her what I told you. I want to apologize and give back her things."

"Matt—please tell me the truth. Did you find Melanie at her apartment, conk her over the head, and leave her there with a concussion and broken leg?"

"Absolutely not. Poor Mel. Is she okay?"

Izzy told Matt what happened, and about Melanie taking care of her friend although she was hobbling around on crutches. "She's fine now, but she had some bad moments, and the leg took a long time to heal. So that little mystery is yet to be solved."

"I'm so sorry to hear that Melanie was hurt. I wonder who conked her, she doesn't have any enemies. This whole thing is a nightmare. I'll be glad when it's all straightened out. I need to return Dwayne's gun too, and apologize to him and his family. Then I need to talk to my parents. I've been trying to call them, but don't get an answer. They may have taken the kids to Disneyland."

That was Izzy's opening and she took a deep breath. "Matt, there's something I have to tell you about your parents. You're right. They're not home. Your father and the children are with Craig. But your mother—Matt, your mother is dead. She died a week ago of a heart attack."

Matt looked at Izzy in disbelief. "No, that's not possible. Mom is much younger than Dad, and she's in very good health. There must be a mistake."

Izzy shook her head. She watched Matt's face change as he absorbed the information. "I'm so sorry to have to tell you this. They tried to find you. Craig called Dwayne, but he had the same number Craig already had. They called everywhere and left messages for you, but when they weren't returned, they finally had to bury her. When Dwayne heard the story, he invited all of them to come to the ranch after the funeral to get their bearings and figure out what to do next. That's where they are now. Craig is taking care of the kids."

The waiter came and picked up the check. "Do you need change?" he asked.

"No, that's okay." Izzy stood up. "Come on, let's go. We can sit in the car and talk."

Matt seemed stunned, and she led him out of the restaurant. "The kids—how are the kids? He started to cry. They're still so young. This is all my fault. I killed her. She shouldn't have had to take on so much responsibility. And my father, he was completely dependent on my mother."

"Don't Matt. You mustn't beat yourself up. Your mother's death wasn't your fault. She must have had heart disease. Alcoholism is a disease too. You must know that from your AA meetings. What's important is that you not let it bring you down, and that you keep your resolve never to take a drink again."

"I won't. Believe me I'll never go there again. Let's see, I've got to think. So they're all at the ranch. Say, would you mind driving, I'm not doing so well here." He handed her the keys, and they changed places."

Izzy decided to wait to tell the rest until after they were back at the apartment. When they got there, Matt went into the bathroom. She could hear him crying over the sound of running water. After a few minutes, she knocked on the door. "Matt, are you okay."

"Just a minute. I'm just going to wash my face." A few more minutes passed, and Matt came out and sat down next to Izzy on the sofa. "Sorry about that. Mom was such a good person. I guess my next step is clear, everyone I need to talk to except Melanie is at the ranch."

Izzy fidgeted. "Well, um, actually, Mel is there too. What you saw when you saw her and Dwayne at the ranch developed into a heavy-duty romance. They've been an item ever since they met, and they just got engaged."

Matt was quiet as he digested this last bit. "You know, I'm not surprised. They're much more suited to each other than we were. Dwayne's more athletic. He plays tennis and swims, and he's certainly more stable than I am. Melanie is like that too. I'm sad for me, but really, I'm happy for them."

Izzy took Matt's hand. "I'm so glad to hear you say that. You know, you're not so bad after all. I have to tell you, when you came in waiving that pistol, I didn't know who to be more afraid of, you or Bruce."

Matt laughed. "I'm sure you'd heard plenty about me to make you feel that way. The truth is, there's a monster inside me who gets out when I drink. He's a whole different person the than one sitting here today. Melanie knew both sides, so I'm not surprised that she fell out of love with me."

"Well the good news is, you never have to let that other person out again. You can build a whole new life with who you are now."

Matt nodded. "Yes, and the first thing I'm going to do is get a job, and set up a decent household so I can take care of my family. Dad's a good man, but he can't get around well with his lame leg, and he's been getting more forgetful over the years. Mom took care of all three of them. They're going to be my responsibility from now on." A tear escaped, and Matt grabbed a tissue from the box on the table.

The phone rang. It was Officer Cruz. " I asked around about Bruce's chances of getting bail. Everyone here seems to think he'll get it. He's had no priors. The first complaint you made didn't hold water. I asked him what happened. He said you told him to tie you up and cut you, some kind of kinky sex thing you liked. He said your friend came in and jumped to the wrong conclusion. He's hired a hard-nosed attorney who has a reputation for winning. He's furious that you accused him of rape, and that your friend knocked him out and tied him up, so be careful. It might be a good idea for both of you to get out of town for a while."

Matt saw Izzy's face change as she listened. "Okay, thanks Officer. We might do that." Izzy felt a knot in her stomach, and her hand trembled as she put down the phone. "Bruce made up a story that I wanted him to tie me up and cut me. He's hired a lawyer who wins all his cases. I can't believe he'd lie like that. Cruz said he'll probably make bail. He suggested we get out of town for a while. He said Bruce was furious with both of us." Izzy's eyes filled with tears. "This is too much. I need to figure out what to do. I can't think of where I could go. You're in danger too, Matt."

Matt sat down next to Izzy and put his arm around her. They were both deep in thought when the phone rang. Izzy picked it up.

"Hi, it's Melanie. I'm so glad you decided to stay at my apartment. How's it going with the writing?"

Izzy's voice quivered, and the tears started again. "Oh, Mel, everything is falling apart. So much has happened, I don't where to begin. I feel like I'm living the worst chapter in my book. Bruce followed me here and tied me to the bed. He hit me, and cut me with a kitchen knife. He tried to rape me again, and he lied to the police. He told them I wanted him to do those things, so he'll probably be out on bail by tomorrow. Mel, I'm terrified of him. Matt's here. He rescued me. He rang the doorbell just in time. He hit Bruce over the head and tied him to a chair. He's in danger too. I know this isn't making any sense, but the police said it would be best if we left town for a while, and I can't think of where I could go."

"Wow! Just a minute. Hold on, I want to talk to Dwayne for a minute." Melanie told Dwayne what Izzy had said. "Matt's with her. He's the one who rescued her from Bruce's attack. The police said Bruce may be out on bail tomorrow, and he might come after both of them. Should we invite them to come here? What do you think? Wait—let me ask Izzy something. Hey Izzy, tell me about Matt. Is he sober?" Melanie held the phone so Dwayne could hear.

"He hasn't had a drink for several months. He's just finishing treatment at a halfway house, and he goes to AA. He said he didn't wack you in your apartment. I believe him, so that bit is still a mystery. Matt came here to apologize, and to bring your things back. If he hadn't come along and heard me screaming, I'd have been raped, and maybe killed. Mel, I told Matt about his mother, and he's heartbroken. I told him about you and Dwayne too. He's okay with that. He wants to get a good job so he can take care of his family again."

Dwayne spoke up. "Hi Izzy, I'm on the phone too. Why don't you both come and stay at the ranch for a while. Bruce will never be able to find you here. It's far away, and he has no connection with us."

"Let me ask Matt." Izzy told him what Dwayne had proposed, and Matt took the phone.

"Hi Dwayne, thanks for asking us. Neither of us knows what to do next. I'm so sorry about everything. I behaved like a jackass, but I can assure you I will never drink again. Izzy told me about you and Melanie. Congratulations. I'm happy for both of you. My Mom's death is a real blow. I want to see my kids and Dad, and apologize to you and Melanie."

"Hey, you two pack up and get out of there. Bruce sounds like bad news. We can figure things out when you get here. Don't tell anyone where you're going, or when you're going to leave."

Matt sounded relieved. "Okay, and thanks for everything, especially for taking my family in. Are they okay? How are the kids?"

"They're doing fine. They were upset at first, but they're coming around now. There's a lot for them to do here, and that helps. Your dad is having a problem accepting that your mother is dead. His memory comes and goes. Melanie thinks he's still in shock, and we're hoping he'll improve with time. Come as soon as you can. Its better if you're not there when that jerk gets out."

"Thanks again Dwayne. We'll leave as soon as we can."

Matt put the phone down and he and Izzy came together and held each other for a long time. Neither of them said a word. Izzy finally broke away. "How far away is the halfway house?"

"It's about half an hour from here."

Izzy paced back and forth. "Matt, I don't want to stay here alone. I've never been so scared in my life. Rhonda's away, her daughter just had a baby. Will you stay here in the guestroom tonight? I'll pack up my clothes and laptop, and we can leave early in the morning. That will get us out of town before the courthouse opens."

Matt frowned. "I'm very familiar with the guestroom. I spent many nights there when I was drunk, and Melanie locked me out of the bedroom. Your plan sounds great. I don't think you should be alone tonight either. The halfway house won't have a problem with my going under these circumstances. I'll have to explain what's going on, but I won't give names or places."

Matt made his call, and Izzy went to find a blanket and pillow. They set the alarm for four. As soon as it went off, they got dressed, put Izzy's things in the car, and drove to the halfway house. Matt tossed some things in a suitcase, and they were out of there and on the highway by five.

Chapter 26 - Jail

Bruce was herded into a big room with a long table and chairs. He was left to cool his heels. Officers Cruz and Draper came in. "We're going to tape the interview. Is that okay with you?" Bruce nodded.

The two officers questioned him over and over again. They finally left, and a third officer came in and asked the same questions. Bruce tried to keep his story straight. He'd primed himself to keep cool, and say as little as he could get away with. He knew what to do from all the years he'd practiced law, but being on the other side of the table was a different story. With his own head in the noose, the stress was getting to him. They left him alone for what seemed like hours. Then the arresting officers came in and grilled him all over again.

Bruce was tired and hungry, and he had to pee. He was sick of answering the same questions. The officers probed until Bruce revealed the loss of his erection when Matt rang the doorbell. Embarrassment turned to anger. He got ornery and started to slip up, forgetting details about the story he'd conjured up. They finally finished questioning him, and booked and fingerprinted him. Bruce was told he could make one phone call. The officer led him to a desk in a corner with a phone and a directory. He called his attorney friend, Jake Bentley, and explained the situation. He told him he was innocent, and had just been doing what the girl said she wanted. Bentley said he'd see what he could do, and would be there in the morning. Bruce looked around. The officers were all busy talking and shuffling paper. He punched in another number. "Hey Jackson? It's Bruce. I need another favor. I want you to tail someone for me."

Chapter 27 – Reunion

Matt and Izzy brought bottled water from the house, and everything she'd bought at Trader Joes. They drove straight through, snacking on yogurt and cookies. When they got to the ranch, they called Dwayne, and he told him how to open the gate. Matt pushed the button, and they took a deep breath as the gate closed behind them.

Dwayne showed them where to park the car. "Hello Matt." Dwayne said. "I'm so sorry about your mother. It's good to see you. Too bad it's under such rotten circumstances. You're looking good though. He put his hand out to Matt, then changed his mind and caught him in a hug." Matt hugged him back.

Craig stepped up and put his hand out to Matt. "Hey, Matt. I'm sorry about Nancy. Caught us all by surprise. We miss her already. But look at you! You finally did it. I'm really proud of you. I quit drinking too. I haven't had a drop for two years now."

Matt shook Craig's hand. "Hi bro. Hey, that's great. Thanks for taking care of my family. I really owe you. Gosh it's so good to see you. I owe all of you an apology. I know I've caused you all kinds of trouble over the years, and here I am again, showing up like a bad penny. I promise you this time I'm going to make things right. Where are the girls?"

"They're up at the barn playing with the kittens." Dwayne turned to Izzy. "I'm so happy to finally meet you. I've heard so much about you from Mel. Here, I'll take those." He took the bags of groceries. Matt and Izzy took their suitcases and followed him into the house.

Matt saw his father sitting on the sofa and went over to him. "Dad, I heard the news about Mom, I'm so sorry." He sat down beside him, and put his hand on his arm.

Lawrence looked at Matt with a glimmer of recognition. "Matthew, you're here. It's so good to see you son. My, you've gotten tall. Your mother will be happy to see you too." Matt hugged his father, and let the tears roll down his cheeks.

Tom put his hand on Matt's shoulder and whispered. "He's okay. He's still in shock, but he's doing a lot better now."

Melanie grabbed Izzy in a hug and brought her into the kitchen. Izzy retold what had happened, filling in the details. Melanie frowned. "You have really been through it! I'm so glad you came. I'm sure you'll be safe here. Can you stay for a while?"

"I can stay until the trial, and I think Matt can too." Izzy brightened a little. "There was just one incident in this whole business with a little humor in it. She told about Bruce's downfall when the doorbell rang, and they burst into laughter. Dwayne came in to find out what happened, hoping there was one piece of good news buried in the story. Melanie hugged her friend again, and they joined the others.

Melanie took Dwayne's hand and led him over to Matt. "We're really glad you came. Sounds like you've been through some pretty heavy stuff. I'm so glad to hear about your recovery program. Izzy said she told you about me and Dwayne. We're going to be married."

Matt stood up. "I'm happy for you, and wish you the very best. Gee, my two best friends are getting married." Another tear squeezed out, and Matt wiped it away. "Where are Susan and Julie?"

"They're in the barn playing with the kittens. Come on, I'll show you. Izzy, do you want to come? They're really cute." They went up the hill to the barn, and paused at the door to watch the children. They had set up a tea party on the hay. Susan had Pops on her lap and was scolding her. "Now you're the biggest and smartest, so you should know better." She turned and saw Matt. It took a moment to register, then "Daddy, Daddy!" she cried, and ran to him. Matt scooped her up in a hug. Julie followed, and Matt kneeled so he could hug both of them.

Jody went over to Izzy. "Hello, I'm Jody, Tom's sister. I'm so glad you're here. Melanie has told us so much about you, I feel like we're already friends. I'm sure you'll be safe here. We're kind of tucked away in the woods."

Izzy looked around. "You really are, and I sure appreciate your taking us in. You know, I've written about things like this happening to other people, but I never dreamed I'd be the one being pursued."

Jody looked at her watch. "Are you hungry? I could sure use a cup of real tea." Jody laughed, pointing to the tea party laid out for the kittens.

Izzy patted her stomach. "I'm starving. We didn't want to stop anywhere, so we've been living on yogurt and junk food all day."

"Well come on back to the house then, all of you. Luz will fix us some sandwiches."

Matt took hold of Julie and Susan's hands and Jody led them back to the ranch house. Susan asked question after question, but Julie chattered non-stop so Matt didn't have a chance to answer any of them.

Luz had anticipated everyone would be hungry, and had set out a platter of sandwiches and a bowl of potato chips. She put a sandwich on a plate and handed it to Matt saying, "You're looking good, but you need fattening up." Everyone laughed.

Tom and Ida filled Matt in on what had been happening since the Walters family had arrived. Tom told him about the church service, and what Lawrence said when he'd become lucid during the circle ceremony. Matt stood up. "I want to express my thanks to all of you for inviting my family to come here, and for taking such good care of them. I am deeply sorry for all the trouble I've caused, and promise to make it up to all of you. I've been in a halfway house, and have a good start on kicking this thing. I'm going to find a job so I can take care of my family."

Susan interrupted. "Daddy, how come you live in half a house? Did someone cut it in two?"

Matt laughed. "No sweetheart. It's a long story. I'll tell you about it later."

Ida came around the table and put her hand on Matt's arm. "The family has talked it over. We'd like you and Lawrence and the girls to stay here until this thing blows over and you get on your feet. Craig, you can stay too, if you like."

Craig hugged Ida. "Thanks, but I've got to get back to work, and I have a girl waiting for me back home."

Matt took a deep breath. "I would like to take you up on that for a while. It would give me time to get a job, and a house near a good school. I can't thank you enough."

Tom got up. "Your recovery is thanks enough, Matt. Izzy, you should stay here too. There's plenty of room to put you all up."

Izzy's face relaxed a little. "I'd sure appreciate hiding out here for a couple of days. And that will give Mel and me a chance to catch up on all those missed phone calls."

Jody moved her things back into her room, and they settled Matt in the bedroom next to the girls. Tom picked up Izzy's suitcase. "Izzy, you can stay in Sharon's room. We put the lamps and toy box in the kids' room, but everything else is intact." Tom opened the bedroom door. The room was beautifully furnished with a queen-sized bed, and a white dresser and desk. Sharon's doll collection and a bookcase of her favorite books were still in place.

Izzy put her laptop on the desk. "This is great. You have no idea how much this means to me. I was scared out of my wits, and really had no other place to go. Rhonda was gone and …" The events of the last couple of days overwhelmed her, and she burst into tears.

Jody put her arm around her. "You poor dear, you certainly have been through a lot. You go ahead and cry, get it out of your system." She stayed with Izzy until she stopped crying. "After this is all resolved, you should think about getting some counseling. It's best to talk about these things to a professional."

"That's a good idea, but what would really make me feel better is to see Bruce behind bars."

Craig announced that he wanted to get back as soon as possible now that everyone was taken care of. "I'll get a red-eye back. Thanks again to you folks for all that you've done." He drew Matt aside. "You know bro, it would be good if you found an AA group here. Kicking that stuff is hard to do on your own, even with the people you have here to support you."

"I was thinking about that too. I'll look in the phone book. There's probably a group that meets in a church or school in the evenings. Don't worry though, the thought of losing my kids again is a huge motivation to stay dry."

"Way to go." Craig patted Matt on the back and went to find a phone.

Chapter 28 - Jackson

Jackson sat slumped behind the wheel of a faded red Chevy truck across the street from the apartment building Bruce told him to stake out. A cigarette hung out of his mouth. He was cold and hungry. He was still pissed that he owed Bruce, and had to be at his beck and call. This is the last time, he thought to himself. I have to put an end to this, or he's going to get me in real trouble. Damn, I really wanted to finish that other job. He dozed off, and woke up to find his leg had fallen asleep. He wiggled and stretched, then looked at his watch. 4:20am.

As he tried to find a more comfortable position, Jackson saw a blond man come out of the building carrying two grocery bags. A tall, good-looking brunette followed. She had a suitcase in one hand, and a laptop case in the other. They put the things in the trunk of a blue Honda Civic and drove off. Jackson waited a minute, then started the engine and followed. They turned onto the highway, and Jackson dropped back a little so he could keep them in sight. He looked at his gas gauge—half a tank. That should get him wherever they were going. Half an hour later, the Honda pulled off the highway and drove to a large three-story house. They parked in front and went inside, than reappeared ten minutes later with another suitcase. They got back onto the highway. Four hours later they were still on the road.

Jackson looked at his gas gauge. It was on empty, and the red light was on. He swore out loud. "Damn it all, if I stop for gas, I'm going to lose them. Where in hell are they going anyway? Well, I have to pull off and fill up. Maybe I can catch up with them." He took the next off ramp and pulled into a gas station. He filled the tank and used the restroom. He bought a coke and an apple turnover, and got back on the highway. He pushed the speed limit and, several miles up, caught up with the Honda.

Chapter 29 – Craig

Craig called the airline, than went to find Matt. "There's a flight out late tonight. Come take a walk with me. I think I left my water bottle in the woods. Say, are you going to be all right with this, taking on the girls and your dad and everything? I'll stay another day or two if you want me to."

"Thanks, but I'll be fine. The Hathaways are great with the kids. They've completely won them over. And as for Dad, it's just going to take some time for him to get over this. As long as he has his books and the family around him he'll be okay, so you go ahead. I'm just happy to have a place to land for a while. That Bruce is a mean bastard, and what a liar! I can't believe the whoppers he told the police."

Craig stopped and turned to his friend. "Yeah? Tell me what happened. I just heard bits and pieces."

Matt told the whole story, ending with the call from Cruz warning them they were in danger and should leave town. Craig scowled. "Wow. It's good you got away. Poor Izzy, what a terrible experience this has been for her. She seems like a nice person. Did you know her before?"

"She's been friends with Melanie for years. She writes crime novels—good ones too. She's published two of them. She brought her laptop with her to work on her latest. She met this guy when she was on vacation in Laguna. She said he was nice at first, but he metamorphosed into a monster."

"So you left the apartment about 4:30. Did you see anyone outside, or any car following you?"

Matt thought for a moment. "It was 4:20 or 4:30, something like that. We set the alarm early. You know, I didn't notice anyone, but we weren't expecting Bruce to be on the loose that early. We figured he would be detained at least overnight."

Craig lit a cigarette. "What kind of traffic was on the road?"

"Traffic was light until we got on the highway, then it was mostly commuters and trucks. It's hard to know if someone's following you on the freeway because everyone's going about the same speed. Do you think we should be concerned?"

Craig started walking again so Matt couldn't see his face. "No, I think I've just got the willies about this whole thing. I'm sure you're safe here, it's so out of the way."

Craig put his clothes in his travel bag and he and Matt joined the family for dinner. Later that evening, he said goodbye to everyone and got in his car. He drove down the driveway and out the gate, than got out of the car to press the button. The big gate swung in an arc, and clanged shut behind him. He looked around to see if there was a road going around the ranch, but couldn't find one.

Craig drove slowly. About a quarter of a mile down, he saw a narrow dirt road and turned onto it. It led to a hiking trail. The trees were thick in that area, and a sign said "Private Property—Do Not Enter." Craig backed out and parked in a thicket of brush across the road. He took his sleeping bag and went to see where the footpath led. It seemed to be headed back to the ranch. After about two miles, he found himself in the woods where he'd spent the night behind cabin nine. It was nearly dark. The woods were quiet except for a few squirrels scampering around, and the occasional caw of a crow.

Craig found a well-hidden spot and unrolled the sleeping bag, fishing out the large bottle of water he'd stuffed in there. He took a swig, and relaxed with his back up against a tree. I'm probably nuts to be doing this, he thought. There's no way the police would have let him go this soon. Yet something about the situation bothered him, and there was too much at stake to let it go. His flight wasn't until two, and it was only an hour to the airport. He decided to hang out in the woods for a while. He dozed off, than awoke with a start. Aauwooo. The coyotes were back, but they weren't in sight.

Craig got up and yawned, than looked toward the cabin. There was a light in the window! Prickles marched up and down Craig's back, and his hands turned clammy. It was way too late for the maid to be cleaning, and he remembered Tom saying they wouldn't put any guests in that unit until they were sure they'd scared off the coyotes. He looked around for a weapon. The rocks on the ground weren't big enough to be of any use. The heaviest thing around was the bottle of water he'd brought with him. He couldn't decide whether to approach the cabin, or watch from a distance.

A figure came around from the front of the cabin, a short heavy man with an uneven gait. Craig couldn't make out his face, but it was definitely not Bruce, who Matt said was tall and about thirty. The man looked at the pond, than walked toward Craig. He puffed on a cigarette, and a trail of smoke followed him. Craig held his breath. The man unzipped his pants and aimed his stream at a tree, then cursed as the urine rolled downhill onto his boot. Craig caught himself smiling in spite of his fear. It was a fate men shared when they weren't used to the woods and didn't check out the lay of the land. A squirrel scampered across a log near Craig. It landed on a pile of leaves. The man jumped and looked up, then started to walk toward Craig again. Craig stood at attention, ready to defend himself with the bottle of water. The man craned his neck. Not seeing anything, he turned and walked back towards the cabin. In a few minutes the light went off.

"That sonofabitch, he's using the cabin as a stake out. What nerve!" Craig tried to control his anger. He knew he had to keep cool to figure out what to do. He didn't know how strong the man was, or whether Bruce was in there with him. He contemplated rushing them, but knew he couldn't handle both of them at once. He decided to go around to the main house to warn the others. He rolled up his sleeping bag and walked deeper into the woods, then left the trail and walked up and around the cabins. He didn't come back to the road until he was almost to the ranch house.

The house was dark except for the suite Dwayne and Melanie stayed in. Matt opened the gate, and walked across the deck towards the door. He was suddenly caught in a stranglehold. As he struggled to get free, he saw a fist coming toward him. He felt a blow to his temple, and blacked out. After a minute, he tried to open his eyes. His vision was blurred and stars danced in front of his eyes. He tried to lift his head, but pain hit him like a hammer, and he lay back down. Someone put a cool wet cloth on his forehead. "Dude, are you okay? Hey, buddy, talk to me. I'm sorry, I didn't know it was you!"

Craig opened his eyes and saw Dwayne looking at him. "Hey, man, you really pack a wallop. Heaven help anyone that tries to go after you." After a few minutes he remembered what happened and sat up. "There's someone in cabin nine. I had a hunch something might go wrong, so I parked the car and hiked in. I watched from the woods and saw a light in the cabin. A short, older man came out. He went into the woods and peed. He heard a squirrel and started to walk toward me—scared me to death because I didn't know what he might try. He didn't see me though. He just went back into the cabin and shut off the light. I didn't know if he was alone, or if that bastard Bruce was in there with him. I didn't think I could handle both of them, so I came back here to warn you and call the police."

Dwayne looked for the card Officer Chavez had given him. He punched in the number and got an answering service. He hung up and called 911. Someone picked up immediately. "This is 911, is this an emergency?"

"Definitely yes."

The operator took Dwayne's name and address, and Dwayne explained what was going on. He was immediately transferred to the Sheriff's office, and explained the situation to them. "Lock up your house. Check all the doors and windows. Is there a way directly to the cabin by car?"

"There is, but they'd hear you, and could escape through the woods. If you go around the back though, there's a footpath to the cabin. You might be able to catch them by surprise. Be careful, it's dark out there."

The officer relayed the message, than said to Dwayne, "Okay now. you all lock up and stay put. Nobody try to play hero, understand? A unit will be there in a few minutes."

Dwayne locked the door to the deck, and checked the windows in the east wing. Melanie checked the front and back doors, and the windows in the living area. Dwayne woke Tom and Ida and told them what was going on. They got up and threw some clothes on, then went to tell Jody and Izzy.

Tom closed the door to Lawrence's bedroom. "Let's let Lawrence and the kids sleep. No sense upsetting them if we can help it. Hopefully, they'll pick up those jerks at the cabin, and we won't have to deal with them at all, but just in case ..." Tom got the key and unlocked the gun cabinet. He gave the pistol to Dwayne and took the revolver, then pointed to the rifle. "Do you know how to use one of those?" he asked Matt.

Matt shook his head. "No sir, I don't."

"I do." Melanie took the rifle, pointed it away from the others, and looked to see if it was loaded. "I took shooting lessons some years ago when we had some robberies in the neighborhood."

Jody shivered. "Well, I do hope you won't have to use those things. My goodness, it's just like *Murder She Wrote!*" Ida pulled the shade in the kitchen window. They turned off all the lights in the house, and sat down to wait. Minutes passed.

Auowooo. Everyone jumped. Craig put his finger to his lips. "It's just the coyotes," he whispered. "I heard them earlier in the woods."

Ten minutes went by, but it seemed like hours. Everyone's nerves were on edge. Izzy looked like she was ready to have a breakdown. Matt sat down next to her and took her hand. "Its okay Iz, they're gonna get him."

Tom went to check the kids. "They're fine," he whispered. "Lawrence was up, but dazed. I told him to go back to sleep."

A few more minutes passed. There was a noise outside, and a rustling of leaves. Izzy held Matt's hand tighter. Everyone turned their attention to where the sound had come from. They heard footsteps coming toward the house. It was quiet for a minute. Then a rock came flying through the kitchen window. Glass flew everywhere, and a hand found its way through the window. The hand cleared the glass away, then felt around and unlatched the window. Matt put his arm around Izzy, and put his finger to his lips. Tom, Dwayne and Melanie stood at attention, their guns aimed at the window.

The man started to pull his way inside, than stopped as he heard footsteps behind him. A low-pitched voice called out "Stop thief!"

Matt stiffened. "That sounds like Dad! He must have gone out the back door. Come on—he could get hurt."

Matt and Dwayne headed out the side door, and walked quietly through the garage. They circled around and came up behind Mr. Walters, who was waving his cane at the burglar. Matt grabbed his father's arm to hold him back. Dwayne poked the live end of his gun between the intruder's shoulder blades. "Okay you—get away from that window and put your hands on your head."

The man jumped down and scrambled around, trying to get away. Everyone held their breath for what seemed like forever, than let it out as they heard two officers running up the road. They grabbed the man, and threw him roughly to the ground. The man struggled, and an officer grabbed his arms and handcuffed his wrists together behind his back.

Matt put his arm around his father. "Good job, Dad."

Tom opened the front door, and the officers half dragged the intruder into the house. Izzy blanched when she saw him. "This isn't the man we were expecting. Bruce is taller, and much younger. Was there anyone with him?"

"No ma'am. He was alone. He had a gun though, and we found a knife in his boot." He turned to the man and growled. "What's your name man."

"My name's Jackson."

"What business do you have with these folks? What were you doing in their cabin, and why are you breaking into their house?" Jackson was silent.

One of the officers took hold of the front of Jackson's shirt and nearly lifted him off the ground. "Now listen you. You'd better start talking, or things are going to get really nasty—hear?"

"Okay, okay, but put me down." Jackson's face was getting red. "I'm just here to do a job. I'm just doing what I was told, that's all, just a job."

"Who sent you here? Who's your boss?" The officer put his face in Jackson's. He raised a threatening hand. "Git talkin' now, my patience is wearing thin."

Jackson squirmed. "Someone did me a favor a long time ago. He keeps asking me to do jobs for him. I tried to tell him I'd had enough, but he wouldn't listen. He thinks I'm his hit man forever because of one little favor."

"And what's this guy's name? Who sent you here tonight?"

"I can't tell you. he'll kill me."

The officer grabbed Jackson again. "Listen you, you're already in a lot of trouble. Now talk!"

"Okay, okay, but he'll kill me. You'll see. He'll find me, or send someone else to do the job. Oh, what's the use, it looks like I'm going to rot in jail anyway."

Just then, Susan and Julie came in, rubbing sleep from their eyes. They saw the officer roughhousing Jackson. "What happened?" Susan cried. "I heard a crash."

Julie spotted the gun Dwayne had left on the kitchen table. She picked it up. "Hey look, just like on TV."

"Julie, no, stop! Put the gun down," Matt shouted. Julie jumped and her finger hit the trigger. The gun went off with a bang, shattering the other kitchen window. Everyone jumped. Mr. Walters ran over and took the gun from Julie, who started to cry.

Ida and Melanie scooped the girls up and carried them into the bedroom. They sat them on the bed and explained as best they could about what had happened. But the night's activities had been more than the girls could take. They had come to feel that the ranch was a haven, and this violence was unexpected. Now it seemed like the entire world was an unfriendly place.

Ida lifted Julie onto her lap. She gave her the Teddy Bear, and rocked her until she finally fell asleep. Susan had a million questions. She held on to the grandma doll until she was finally satisfied that everyone was safe. Melanie tucked her in with the doll in her arms, and stayed until she was asleep.

The officers continued to question Jackson, but they were getting nowhere. He kept dodging their questions. They read him his rights, and were preparing to haul him off to jail when he finally broke.

"Okay— okay. I'll squeal. It's my lawyer, Bruce Anderson. He got me off a couple of years ago, and now he keeps asking me to do his dirty work. I tried to quit, but he won't let me. He says he'll have me killed if I don't do what he wants. Honest. I didn't want to hurt anyone." Jackson sniffed, and wiped his nose on his shirt sleeve.

Izzy nodded. "That's the man who attacked me, Bruce Anderson. He was arrested yesterday for cutting me, and trying to rape me. We hoped he'd be kept overnight, but he must have been released on bail." The officer took notes as Izzy told the rest of the story.

Mr. Walters went over to Jackson, waving his cane at him. "Now you listen here Mr. Jacks, or whoever you are. Don't you ever come around here again, bothering my family. I won't stand for it." Jackson laughed at him and kicked his cane out of his hands. Matt, Dwayne and Craig tackled Jackson and wrestled him to the floor.

Jody cheered them on. "Lordy be, it's *Murder She Wrote* and the 49ers football game, all on the same night. What fun!" The officers grabbed Jackson, and the men got up. Melanie hugged Jody, and Dwayne patted her on the back. "Only you would find humor in a night like this Jody, bless your heart."

Part VII

Epilogue

Dwayne and Melanie were married in the chapel. They stayed at the Bar None Dude Ranch after they were married. As Tom and Ida began to slow up, they took over running the ranch. Their twins, Jeremy and Lisa, brought joy to the whole family. When Tommy's parents went back on drugs, Tommy was taken back into social services, and Dwayne and Melanie took him in again. They eventually became his guardians, than adopted him when there was no possibility of his parents regaining custody. Tommy's parents were welcome at the ranch as long as they stayed sober. They visited often, and were included in all the holiday and birthday get-togethers.

Ida stayed on her medication, and continued to get regular check ups with Doctor Elmer. Her efforts were rewarded with many years of good health. She continued to enjoy her children and grandchildren, and her warm relationship with Tom and the other family members.

Tom was delighted to find that Lawrence was a wiz at checkers. They played often, and Lawrence taught Tom all his secret tricks and strategies. The next time he and Ida visited the Ellisons, Tom surprised everyone by winning every game.

Jody and Lawrence became close friends. They spent many hours talking about old times, and Lawrences quick wit matched Jody's. He could beat her in gin, scrabble and checkers, but every once in a while he called her Nancy.

Lawrence was very intelligent and highly educated. He had memorized poems and passages from the many books he'd read. He loved to quote from Shakespeare, and could recite whole passages from Steinbeck's stories. Lawrence's short-term memory continued to wane slightly, but he clearly remembered things that had happened long ago. When Matt took the children, Lawrence chose to stay at the ranch.

Sharon and Jeff visited the ranch often. Jeff became attached to Ginger, a beautiful horse that Lance had broken and trained. In spite of Lance's training, Ginger had a mind of her own. No one at the ranch had been able to ride her, but Jeff loved a challenge. He was thrown a couple of times, but got right back on. With Lance's help, Jeff soon had Ginger responding to him almost as well as Penny did to Sharon. They rode whenever they visited, and often joined Dwayne and Melanie on their rounds of the ranch in the morning.

Matt and Craig sold most of their stock when the market was at its peak. They were both heavily invested in technology, and their investments had grown far beyond their expectations. They bought two large houses with the money, and turned them into halfway houses for recovering alcoholics. The stock market bubble broke some time later. The stock they'd kept lost half its value, but the market eventually began to recover.

Craig quit smoking and stayed sober. He married his girlfriend, and they visited the ranch often to see his godchildren. They bred show dogs, and gave Dwayne and Melanie a toy poodle puppy, which Goldie immediately adopted.

The entire family helped care for Susan and Julie until Matt was able to take them back. The girls were traumatized by the events they'd experienced. Dwayne and Melanie were their primary caregivers. They took them to counseling, which helped somewhat, but they had nightmares for a long time. The girls were very bright.

Matt stayed single for a time. He didn't date, or try to meet anyone, because he was afraid his past would prevent nice women from wanting to hook up with him. He finally fell in love with someone who had checked into the halfway house. They got married, and bought a beautiful house in Northern California where they made a home for Susan and Julie.

Susan continued to take ballet lessons, and learned to play the piano by ear. She learned all the oldies, and played for the residents of the local senior home. She majored in cardiology in medical school, and graduated at the top of her class.

Julie went to Stanford and joined the cheerleading team. True to her commitment, she always stayed on the bottom. After she graduated, she bought a ranch where she raised and trained race horses. She met her soul mate at the track, and they got married in the chapel at the Hathaways ranch. The reception was—you guessed it—a hoedown

Hilda, Luz and Marcus enjoyed the Hathaways' expanded family, and doted on the children. Luz was offered a job at another ranch for almost double the salary, but she loved the Hathaways, and chose to remain with them.

Hilda stayed active until her 90th birthday. She was finally persuaded to retire when arthritis made it difficult for her to move around. She stayed at the ranch, and everyone waited on her hand and foot. Her lap was Pops' favorite resting place. Pops would meow up at her until Hilda invited her to hop up. Then she'd make her way up to Hilda's chest and carefully place one paw on her right shoulder and the other on her left, in a delightful cat hug. She stayed there purring loudly while Hilda smoothed her thick, orange fur.

Sara and Paula interviewed dozens of massage therapists, but never found anyone to replace Melanie. They continued to run the business themselves until a chiropractor with a large practice invited them to become associates. Sara and Paula were ecstatic, and the merger gave the business a much-needed boost. Paula eventually married the chiropractor. They had five children, and their household also included a parrot, two dogs, and a cat.

Sara opted to stay single. She loved to dance, and went line dancing twice a week. She met a very nice man there who taught her to ballroom dance. They entered a contest and won first prize for the Tango.

Rhonda rented Melanie's apartment to a very nice elderly couple, and they became good friends. They introduced her to their son, Frank, who'd lost his wife several years ago. Rhonda and Frank were immediately attracted to each other, and found they had a lot in common. They were married the following year.

Nettie continued to raise Moesha until she went off to college and got her nursing degree. After she graduated, Moesha got a job near her mother so she could help support her. Her mom finally kicked out her abusive boyfriend when he trashed their house during a drinking binge. Moesha met a very nice boy in one of her classes. Her boyfriend's father, who was a perfect gentleman, took a liking to her mom. They saw each other often and eventually got married.

Lance went to work on Julie's ranch as her lead trainer. He was a wiz at selective breeding, and produced ponies with speed and endurance. He had a knack for breaking colts in a gentle but firm manner, and the horses flourished under his care. Many of the horses he'd trained won first and second place at the track.

Bruce was convicted of five counts of first-degree murder; two counts of rape; two of attempted rape; breaking and entering; and assault and battery. Both his former wife and ex-girlfriend came forward during the trial to testify he'd terrorized and raped them. They'd not filed reports because he'd threatened to kill them. He was sentenced to life imprisonment with no possibility of parole. He contracted HIV in prison, and suffered from lesions and nausea and other illnesses associated with AIDS. Bruce died in prison after serving five years of his term.

Jackson was sentenced to life imprisonment on three counts of first-degree murder, and two counts of assault and breaking and entering. He antagonized the other inmates, and was disliked by the wardens. He was beaten to death in prison when his fellow inmates caught him stealing cigarettes.

Gracie turned out to be a good milk cow. She remained placid, and grew up looking just like Anabelle. She was everybody's favorite, and was pampered by the guests as well as the staff.

George was a magnificent specimen, but continued to have a bad temper. Tommy entered him in 4H, and the bull won first prize, than tried to escape when one of the judges opened a gate. Jody made a purple ribbon to hang on the wall next to his blue one. It was an honorary decree stating that George was the stubbornest, most ornery creature that ever graced the ranch.

Orange Popsicle moved into the main house as soon as she was litter trained. She had her own automated litter box. It had a noisy motor that started up with a racket fifteen minutes after she'd visited it. Pops was entranced with the gadget. Every time she heard the motor, she ran back to the box, walked around it, and watched as the litter lifter circled around, and the rake lifted the clumps. A lid on the box opened, and the rake dumped the clumped litter into a box. Pops watched until the lid closed and the motor stopped. Then she ran through the house, from the east wing to the west, ending in the kitchen, where she skidded across the linoleum and came to a stop at Hilda's feet, meowing energetically until she got a treat.

The mystery of who conked Melanie on the head in her apartment remained unsolved. The police guessed Matt had left the door slightly ajar when he left. They thought someone might have come in, sized up the situation, and decided to clean out the rest of Melanie's things. Then, when Melanie walked in, they were so surprised and rattled, they dropped everything and hit her on the head so they could get away.

Part VIII

Chapter 30 – A Wrap

Izzy undid the sweatshirt she'd tied around her waist. She jogged up the stairs and sat down on the bench on the front porch of her town home. She stayed for a while, watching a pair of doves billing and cooing, then came inside, checked the mail, and poured a cup of coffee. She grabbed a package of chocolate-covered cranberries and sat down at her computer.

Izzy keyed in the last chapter of her novel, reread it and made a few changes, then hit save. She loaded the paper tray, and clicked on print. "That's a wrap," she said out loud as the printer whirred and clicked. "But I don't like all the crying I do in the last chapter. It makes me sound too wimpy. Maybe I'll take that part out, or change my name in the book to Betsy."

Izzy leaned back in her chair and stretched her arms over her head. She let out a big sigh. "Now if I could just meet someone like Dwayne. He's a dreamboat."

Printed in the United States
144438LV00001B/1/P

9 781440 122279